ONE SMALL CLUE

ONE SMALL CLUE

by Mara Kay

CROWN PUBLISHERS, INC.
New York

Library of Congress Cataloging in Publication Data
Kay, Mara.
One small clue.
Summary: When they discover they are the orphaned children
of a Russian stowaway, sixteen-year-old twins Madge and
John travel to the port city of Odessa to try and trace
the one small clue they have of their parents' identity.
[1. Soviet Union—Fiction.   2. Twins—Fiction.
3. Brothers and sisters—Fiction.   4. Mystery and
detective stories]   I. Title.
PZ7.K1980n   [Fic]   82-5057
ISBN 0-517-54615-9   AACR2

CONTENTS

1 | THE DOUBLE BIRTHDAY   1

2 | A STOWAWAY   3

3 | CONVERSATION WITH JOHN   9

4 | THE SEARCH BEGINS   12

5 | PLANS   17

6 | PREPARATIONS   20

7 | FLIGHT TO ODESSA   23

8 | THE DOUGLASES   26

9 | NEW FRIENDS   31

10 | ARKADI   41

11 | TROUBLE   48

12 | THE TWO ARAPOVS   51

13 | VICTOR   57

14 | MISS KELLY   63

15 | UNEXPECTED ENCOUNTER   68

16 | VICTOR'S FATHER   71

17 | SAILOR JOE   75

18 | THE FIRST RIPPLES 80

19 | THE RIPPLES WIDEN 88

20 | THE CHASE 91

21 | A LETTER FROM KSENIA 98

22 | DOWN THE FIRE ESCAPE 101

23 | VIOLA INTERFERES 107

24 | FACE TO FACE 113

25 | HOMEWARD 120

CHAPTER 1

THE DOUBLE BIRTHDAY

SIXTEEN candles on the big birthday cake were burning brightly. The strains of "Happy birthday, dear Madge and John, happy birthday to you" still lingered in the air.

Madge knew that this was the time for her and her twin brother to make a wish and blow out the candles, yet she did not move. Her eyes fixed on her plate, her lips tight, she was fighting a strange feeling of being two people. One person was the carefree Madge Sullivan who lived with her brother John and her grandfather, Patrick Sullivan, in a gray-shingled house on the north shore of Long Island. The second person was also called Madge Sullivan, but—and here the eerie feeling deepened—Madge could not be sure who that person really was.

An awkward silence made Madge look up. All of the guests were staring at her, and across the table John was hissing, "Come on."

A light tapping of crutches approaching the dining room gave Madge a chance to collect her thoughts. She said with relief, "He's coming. Let's wait."

The tall, lanky boy sitting next to her asked, "Your grandfather used to be a sea captain, right?"

Madge nodded. "Yes. He owned a freighter, *Josephine,* and before that there was another one, *The Eagle.*"

"Gosh, his own freighter!" The boy looked impressed, but Madge was not paying any attention to him. She was listening to the sound of the crutches.

1

The Captain had become an invalid when he missed a step on the stairway of his own house and fell. His hip had been broken in two places and his back was injured so badly that for weeks the doctors hadn't been sure whether he would walk again. After several months of therapy, he began to leave his wheelchair, first for just a short time, then for hours. Now he was able to get around on crutches.

Lowering his voice, the boy next to Madge said, "I guess your brother would have liked to step into your grandfather's shoes, but of course he can't."

Madge answered curtly, "No, he can't," and turned away. It bothered her to have anyone mention John's limp. It was hardly noticeable when he walked. Still, it prevented him from taking part in sports. He never talked about it, but Madge knew that he would have liked to play baseball or football. Sometimes he watched school matches, but mostly he stayed at home and read. Perhaps that was what made him so serious. "Very mature for his age," the school principal had once said.

"Here's grandfather!" John exclaimed as Captain Sullivan entered the dining room. He stood by the door, leaning on his crutches. His broad shoulders stooped slightly, but his eyes were still a vivid blue.

Two boys jumped up and offered him their seats. The Captain waved them away. "No, thank you. I just dropped in for a minute to see how the feast was going." He sounded cheerful, but Madge noticed that he looked anxiously first at her, then at John, who answered, "Everything is fine, Granddad. Madge and I were just going to blow out the candles." He glared at his sister and she got up.

"Make a wish! Make a wish!" everybody called.

A wish? Madge thought. Yes, she had one—to have everything just exactly as it had been before ten o'clock that morning. "But that could never be," she murmured to herself, watching the candles go out one by one.

CHAPTER 2

A STOWAWAY

THE party was over. Stretched out on her bed, her hands clasped behind her head, Madge listened to the clock downstairs strike nine. The radiant May day had turned chilly toward evening. She had changed out of her gauzy yellow dress and had turned off the overhead light. The soft glow from her bedside lamp barely touched the posters and photographs of movie stars hanging on the walls.

Closing her eyes, Madge almost drifted into sleep but jerked herself back. No, *no*, it was simply useless to try to escape into dreams. She had to think back, go step by step over the entire day. Perhaps that would make the strange feeling of being two people disappear.

Madge gazed at the ceiling. The morning had begun as usual. . . . No, not quite as usual: There had been excitement in the air. For the first time since the Captain's accident three years earlier, she and John were going to have a real birthday party. They had talked and laughed a lot at breakfast. The table was strewn with gift wrappings and ribbons. There were gifts from the Captain: a new camera for John and a small emerald heart, her birthstone, on a slender gold chain for Madge. Aunt Helen had sent each of them a check for ten dollars to buy something they really wanted. A friend of their grandfather, who was also a sea captain, had sent two little ivory elephants for good luck.

As soon as breakfast was over, the Captain rose from his seat.

"Let's go to the den," he said, "I have something to tell both of you."

Madge remembered with surprise that she had never felt even a twinge of uneasiness as she and John followed the Captain into his den. At the time she had only noticed how her grandfather winced when he lowered himself into the big green leather chair, and that beyond the windows the fog was lifting from the bay.

How had he begun his story? Madge was not sure. Instead of listening, she had been admiring her necklace, holding the emerald to the light. She heard the Captain say something about sailing *Josephine* to Odessa with some machinery for the pier. On their return trip, they had been caught in a storm and the freighter was tossed about badly. Just one of grandfather's sea yarns, Madge had thought, wondering why he had chosen this particular morning to tell one when there was so much to do. Then the Captain had said, "We were within sight of Hoboken, New Jersey, and I was shaving in my cabin, when young O'Malley rushed in shouting that there was a woman hiding in the hold and that she was about to give birth. The first mate and I went to the hold immediately," he continued, "and sure enough there was a young woman, about twenty, maybe a little older, lying on a bed of burlap bags, which was almost hidden by some empty packing cases. She was thrashing about and it was clear at a glance that she *was* about to give birth. Luckily, by that time we were already docking. The pier got in touch with the nearest hospital and the ambulance came within minutes."

"A stowaway!" John exclaimed. "But where did she get on the ship? In Odessa?"

The Captain nodded. "No doubt about it. *Josephine* was not in very good shape. I was planning to put her in dry dock as soon as we reached the States. That's why we didn't stop at any port on our way back. As to how the woman got into the hold, I wouldn't be a bit surprised if it was O'Malley himself who had smuggled her in. He was the youngest and least reliable of the crew, always involved in some monkey business. Besides, he had just been engaged and was sending his girl expensive gifts from every port. He needed money and could be bribed easily. He might never have realized how far along the woman was in her pregnancy."

Strange, Madge thought. Even at that point in the story she had still not seen the truth. John, too, had seemed unconcerned.

"There were at least five inches of water at the bottom of the hold," the Captain continued. "Apparently *Josephine* had sprung a slight leak. Floating in the water was a small wicker basket that must have served as a suitcase. I fished it out and examined the contents, hoping to find some identification of our stowaway. Inside was a dress, a change of underwear, two books and a passport. I examined the passport, but the water had reduced it almost to pulp. All I could decipher was the date of birth, July 1941, and what appeared to be a first name. It looked like 'Maria.' "

The Captain cleared his throat and continued rapidly, as if he were anxious to have the story over. "Later, the head nurse at the hospital told me that Maria had just given birth to twins and"—he paused—"that she was not expected to live. The nurse let me in to see her for a few minutes. She was barely able to speak, but she whispered, 'I wanted my children to be born free.' I asked her if her husband was alive and she nodded. That was all. The nurse said I should leave. Half an hour later, Maria died."

Madge knew that she must have said something, but all she could remember was her brother's voice, low and hoarse. "That woman, Maria, she was our mother, wasn't she? You were telling us about ourselves."

Madge remembered crying at that moment, "No, no! This is just one of your sea stories, grandfather! It can't be true!"

Then John had interrupted. "Sure it's true. Do you think grandfather would make up a story like that?" He was shaking all over, and when Madge looked at her own hands she saw that they were gripping the arms of her chair so tightly that the knuckles were all white. "We are not really your grandchildren then, are we?" she said.

The Captain answered, "No, but I love you both as if you were my own—more perhaps."

Madge turned to John and saw that his eyes were wet. She had not seen her brother cry since they were small children. The next moment she was crying too, her face against the back of her chair.

The Captain sighed. "I did not expect this would upset you both so much, but I had to tell you sooner or later."

What had the Captain said next? Madge could recall only snatches. He had explained how his lawyer had gotten in touch with the Immigration Department and that it had been decided to keep the whole matter as quiet as possible. Even though the twins were American citizens, their father or other relatives might insist on their being returned to Russia. Their demands would probably be refused and then the Russian papers would scream about the American government keeping Russian children away from their family. American papers would pick up the story and the Captain would see no end to journalists and photographers.

"So I decided to wait until you were old enough to understand the situation," he said. "But in the meantime my son died and then I had my accident. Sometimes I wondered if I should tell you that you were adopted at all. You were both so happy and adjusted. But finally I realized I had to do it, and this seemed to be the right day."

"Didn't the hospital people get our mother's last name?" John asked.

"They tried to question her," the Captain explained, "but she was not in a state to answer. Several days in the hold and being tossed around by the waves is not a very good preparation for childbirth. It is a miracle you were both born healthy."

"Except for my leg," John said.

Madge had dug her face deeper into the soft back of the arm-chair and wished that the Captain and John would stop talking. Every word they said made her head ache. But John would not stop asking questions. Now he wanted to know whether Maria spoke in Russian or in English when she said she wanted her children to be born free.

"English with a British accent," the Captain told him. "But she was Russian, no doubt about it. We made out on her passport that she was born in Odessa, and the books she had with her were in Russian."

Madge had begun to wonder what John would ask next when she heard the sound of the Captain's crutch against the floor. He was getting out of his chair and was coming toward her.

"Madge," the Captain said quietly. "Nothing has changed. We are still together, the three of us. Life can go on as usual, except that you both know about your past now."

"But that's just it!" Madge said. "That is what's so frightening! We don't really know anything about our past. Who are we anyway?"

"Oh, stop," John said.

"She's upset." The Captain walked back to his chair then and sat down heavily, shading his eyes with his hand. After a few minutes, he lowered his hand. "Why don't we forget the entire business at least for today? Don't you both have things to do for the party? Winona is probably busy in the kitchen with the cake."

John rose first. "I guess we better go."

They were almost at the door, when the Captain called out, "Wait! I thought you might want these." He held out two books, one blue, the other green. Both were badly water-stained.

John hesitated. "I don't know. If they're in Russian, what's the use?" But Madge said quickly, "Yes, please. I want them."

Later in the dining room John said, "I'm sorry I snapped at you, but I was sort of shook up."

"I know," Madge said. "I know." She was looking at the breakfast table that was still not cleared. It was odd. Only an hour before, she and John had been sitting there, arguing about the color of the birthday candles for the cake, as if it were the most important matter in their lives.

CHAPTER 3

CONVERSATION WITH JOHN

SOMEONE banged at the door and John's voice called, "Madge? Are you in bed already?"

She called back, "No, come in."

John slipped into the room. He looked calm, but as soon as he began to speak, Madge could tell that he was irritated. "Everyone left the party early," he said. "We didn't get a chance to do half the things we were planning."

"I didn't mind," Madge answered. "I wanted to be left alone to think."

"You were thinking all through the party. Didn't you see everybody staring at you?"

"I don't care." Madge stretched and half closed her eyes. "John, do you remember what grandfather said about our mother? Was she slender, with dark hair and eyes? Aren't we like her?"

"I guess so."

"You think so? I'm glad. I want to look like mother. What else did he say? I was crying so hard, I didn't catch everything."

"Well, he only said it wasn't easy for him to adopt us. The authorities wanted us to be placed in a foster home because grandfather was a widower and there wasn't anyone to help him look after us. Hired help wasn't enough they said. But when grandfather told them that his sister was coming, everything was all right."

Aunt Helen . . . The thought of her made Madge smile a little. Aunt Helen had always been on hand to tell stories or to nurse a bruised knee. Winona, the housekeeper, was a great storyteller too. Only she told scary ones. Black-skinned, with the features of an Indian, Winona had both bloods in her and that is why, she said, she was able to "see things." She could also predict the weather more accurately than the radio forecast, which greatly amused the Captain.

"I wish Aunt Helen had stayed on with us," Madge said. "Why did she have to go and get married?"

John laughed. "We were thirteen when she left. We were old enough to be on our own anyway."

"Yes, and old enough to be told the truth about ourselves. Grandfather shouldn't have made us believe we were his son's children."

"Are you for real, Madge?" John said. "*You* made us believe that."

"I never—" Madge began and then stopped. She suddenly had thought of herself, about three or four years old, staring at a photograph of a man in an air force uniform. She had asked Aunt Helen, "Is this our daddy? Where is he? Is he dead like Mommy?" Aunt Helen hadn't answered. Madge had chanted, "It's Daddy! It's Daddy, isn't it? I shall ask Grandpa." Aunt Helen's reaction had been tearful. "No. Please don't talk to your grandfather about him. Yes, he is dead."

Aunt Helen had sounded so firm that Madge obeyed, and John just didn't seem interested. Later they heard about how their grandfather's only son, Richard Sullivan, had crashed during a routine flight when something went wrong with the engine of his plane. Madge and John seldom mentioned Richard's name because it made their grandfather look so sad. There wasn't much time to bother about the past anyway. Their parents were dead. Their mother had died in childbirth and they were living with their grandfather. That was all.

"It used to be so simple," Madge said, "and now we don't know who our parents were." When her brother didn't answer, she said, "I can see this doesn't matter to you. You couldn't care less, right?"

John answered calmly. "I wouldn't say I don't care. It just seems like something you read about in a book. Speaking of which, did you look at the ones Maria had on the ship with her?"

"Yes, I did, but why do you say, 'Maria'? Can't you say 'mother'? She *is* our mother, you know." Sitting up on her bed, Madge glared at John.

"And why did you avoid saying 'grandfather'? Whenever you spoke about him earlier today, it was always 'he.'"

Without answering, Madge took the books off her bedside table and gave them to him.

"Grandfather said that the blue one is the New Testament and the green one is poetry," John said, bending over the books. "Boy, are they in bad shape." The print was half washed away and some of the pages were stuck together. "Well, we can't read Russian anyway."

"I wish there was a name on the flyleaf," Madge said. "But there isn't. John, do you realize that we don't even have a last name?"

"Sure we do. Sullivan."

"Come on! You know what I mean—our *real* name."

"Sullivan is real enough for me." John put the books on the floor and faced his sister. "As far as I'm concerned, the Captain is my grandfather and this house is my home. If you want to go and dig in the past, that's your business."

"Well, don't think that I'm ungrateful, or that I don't care about what grandfather has done for us. We might have been in an orphanage if it hadn't been for him. But I still want to know where we came from."

"Come on—" John began, but Madge shook her head. "It's no use trying to get me to forget the whole thing because I won't." Her throat tightened and she whispered, "Good night. Please go now. I—I want to be alone."

CHAPTER 4

THE SEARCH BEGINS

MADGE was quiet for the next few days. She spent hours curled up in a chair, staring into space, her hands folded in her lap. One day John found her in the Captain's study, slowly turning his giant globe. "Look," she said without glancing up, "there's Odessa. It's a big port on the Black Sea. Lots of foreign ships moor there. It isn't far from the Crimea, but winters are cold and even snowy."

John laughed. "You must have really read up on the subject." Madge did not smile. "Yes, I did," she said. "I'm learning the Russian alphabet, too. I got a book out of the library."

"What for? You're not planning to go to Russia, are you?"

"Why not? Lots of tourists visit Russia. Wouldn't you want to go?"

John shrugged his shoulders. "Oh, I wouldn't mind, but there are other places I'd rather see. The Amazon River, for instance, or Australia, or Scotland."

"Oh, it's simply no use talking to you," Madge said, spinning the globe.

But a few days later she brought up the subject once more. "John, listen," she said, pedaling beside him on the way to school. "You talk about our going to Russia as if we were just tourists out to see the sights and it would be just as good if we went to Australia. Don't you realize that someone in Odessa might be thinking about us and hoping that perhaps one day we would turn up?"

"What are you talking about?" John turned around so sharply, his bicycle almost ran into Madge's. "Oh, I see. . . . You mean Maria's husband."

"I mean our father."

"He may not know we exist."

"I'm sure he does. We were born as soon as Maria arrived here. She must have been with her husband until she left."

"Who knows? Perhaps. Anyway, he wouldn't know there are two of us."

"Yes, he would. Doctors can tell in advance."

John rode silently for a few minutes, then asked abruptly, "Aren't you forgetting the main point?"

"What?"

"We don't have the slightest idea of our father's name."

"We could find out somehow."

"How? We haven't got a single clue."

"A clue. . ." Madge said pensively. "That gives me an idea. . . ."

"Great! Just go ahead and look for one. And watch for that car. It's almost on top of us."

"I *will* look and I will find it," Madge insisted after the car had safely passed.

Her brother did not answer. He went on pedaling faster and faster along the sunlit road.

From that day on Madge spent a lot of time with the two books that were found in the hold of the ship. She handled them continuously, examining every page, trying to pry open the ones that were stuck together.

"Why so much interest in those old books?" the Captain asked one evening, watching as she bent over the New Testament.

"I thought there might be a bookmark, or something between the pages."

The Captain smiled. "Yes, there could be, I suppose. Tell me, does your brother share your interest?"

"John doesn't care."

The Captain nodded. "Thought so." Then he added, wistfully, "Aren't you satisfied with your life here? I used to think you were both happy being with me. I am sure John still is, but you . . ."

"Of course I'm happy with you, grandfather. Who wouldn't be?"

Nothing more was said about the books, but Madge continued to work on the stuck pages. She tried to loosen them, first with a paper knife, then by wetting the edges with a wad of cotton. Page after page came unstuck, but there was nothing between them.

One rainy afternoon Madge was doing her homework at the dining-room table because Winona was spring-cleaning upstairs. At the other end of the table, John mumbled, "There'll be leftovers for dinner tonight. Winona is too busy to cook."

"I guess so," Madge answered, listening to the vacuum cleaner overhead. She finished her geometry problem, stretched, and then reached for the Russian poetry book. The pages she had wet the night before were almost dry and separated easily. She began to turn them one by one, without much hope, and suddenly cried, "John, look!"

John jumped off his chair and hurried over to where his sister was sitting.

Madge held up a blue envelope folded like a bookmark. "There is an address," she said excitedly. "I see it. Perhaps— Oh, John! Just as I was going to give up this whole business."

"Let's see it," John said. He peered at the envelope Madge was flattening on the table. "Good, it's typed."

"But it is in Russian," Madge wailed, staring at the three neatly typed lines. "I only can read one word—*Odessa.*"

"Aren't you learning the alphabet? Try to make this out," John said.

Madge put her finger on the first word. "Mar . . . Maria, I suppose. No, the next letter is . . . is— Got it, *N.* Marina, not Maria. They didn't get her name right at that hospital. Ara . . .

Ara . . . I can't remember that next letter. Wait. Let me get my book."

Madge dug into her schoolbag and pulled out a Russian dictionary. "Here," she said, and thrust it into John's hands. "You check the letters and I'll write them down. The alphabet is right on the first page."

It took some time, but the twins continued letter by letter. "I think we have it," Madge said and read slowly:

> MARINA ARAPOVA
> UYUTNAYA 3,
> ODESSA

"Oh, John, Arapov must be our father's name!"

"Arapov?"

"Yes. Don't you see? The *a* is a feminine ending."

"But how do you know that's Marina's married name?"

"It has to be," Madge said. She pointed to the postmark. "See, it says 1963, the year before we were born."

John nodded. "You're right. Won't grandfather be surprised."

Madge started. "We're not showing this to him." She glanced anxiously at the door. "He isn't at home, is he?"

"No, he's at his club. But I don't get it. Why shouldn't he see it?"

"Because if he does, he might never let us go to Russia. Don't you remember what he said last week? He said that people who go to Russia should behave like tourists, buy souvenirs and look at sights; they shouldn't try to start conversations with the local people or visit private homes. Well, we're planning to do just that—talk to people and go into houses. Of course, if father is still at number 3 Uyutnaya Street, we have no problem. But he might have moved and then we would have to find where to."

"Fat chance finding out anything like that." John looked thoroughly skeptical. "You're out of your mind, Madge."

"I am not and he still might be at that address. The most important thing is that we have his last name. I'm sure he'll be happy to see us. John, seriously, don't you want to find our father?"

John seemed at a loss. He ruffled his hair and mumbled, "Who said we're going to Russia anyway?"

"I'll ask grandfather. After all, he said he would like us to travel and broaden our horizons."

"Then go ahead, but don't be surprised if he offers you a nice vacation in a summer camp instead."

CHAPTER 5

PLANS

MADGE spent a sleepless night trying to think of the best way to approach the Captain about letting her and John go to Odessa. Finally she decided simply to say that they wanted to visit their native country.

At first the Captain would not even discuss the idea. "It is not the expense," he told them. "In fact, I have been thinking of sending you two on a European tour, but after you finish college. You are not old enough to go alone. If I could come with you, it would be different. Perhaps next year, if my hip gets better...."

"But anything can happen between now and next year," Madge wailed. "What if there is another war, or something like that? Oh, grandfather, please let us go."

"I said no, Madge."

"But if we stayed at a good hotel—" John began.

The Captain cut him short. "Youngsters of your age should not be on their own. Let's talk about all this in a few years, all right?"

John nudged Madge. "We can't argue. It will only make things worse."

For the next few days nothing was said about the trip, but Madge's pinched face and tearful eyes began to wear the Captain down. "Since you are both so keen to visit Russia, I thought I would arrange a tour for you," he announced one evening at dinner.

John exclaimed, "That would be great!" But Madge was frantic. "No, grandfather! Going with a tour would mean visiting a lot of places and probably staying for only a couple of days in each one. We want to stay in Odessa, where our mother lived, and—and look around."

"Well," the Captain began, "I was going to suggest that you go to Moscow for a month or so. I have friends in the American embassy there. They could put you up. But Odessa . . . I can't think of anyone I know there. Now, in Leningrad—"

Madge almost shouted, "We don't need Leningrad!"

"Good heavens!" The Captain threw his napkin on the table and asked Winona, who had just appeared in the door, to serve him coffee in the den.

"He's making a phone call," Madge whispered, listening to the sounds coming from the den. "Do you think he's trying to arrange something for us so that we can go to Odessa?"

"Could be. I wish you hadn't refused to go on a tour, though. It would have been better than nothing."

"I had to, John. We would need time to ourselves once we were there."

John lowered his voice. "You mean to look for our father? That's crazy. You know it is."

"All right, so it's insane. Then why do *you* want to go to Russia?"

"I'd like to see the country. It would be a fantastic vacation. . . . I'd use my camera a lot."

"You're—" Madge swallowed her words. The Captain was coming out of the den.

"Good news for you!" he said. "Remember the electrical engineer, Steve Douglas, who used to visit us? Last year his company sent him to Russia to supervise an electrical installation on a pier somewhere in the north. Later, I heard he was transferred to a port on the Black Sea. Well, I just called a friend of his in New York. Steve is in Odessa. He was on leave about six months ago, got married, and returned to Odessa with her. I can't remember her name, but I have their address." The Captain waved a slip of paper. "No harm in writing to him and asking if they wouldn't mind having you two for a few weeks. Steve is responsible. I wouldn't have to worry if you were with him."

"Grandfather, write him at once!" Madge pleaded.

John muttered, "Suppose he says no?"

"I am not even listening to you," Madge said.

CHAPTER 6

PREPARATIONS

TWO weeks later, Steve's answer came. He and his wife would be delighted to have the twins. "I have a couple of conditions you both must meet if you really want to go," the Captain told Madge and John. His conditions were good passing grades at school and their learning some Russian, so an elderly Russian lady was found and lessons began. To Madge's delight, their teacher used what she called the "direct method." At the first lesson, she made the twins memorize the names of items placed on the table and then started to build sentences around them. The lesson was more like conversation than learning dry rules.

"It was fun," Madge told the Captain after the lesson was over, "and we learned a lot."

"It's a good system," John agreed. "It forces us to speak right from the beginning."

"Don't overdo it," the Captain cautioned when he found Madge dozing off in front of the television mumbling Russian words. "I've never seen you put so much effort into homework."

As soon as school let out for the summer, preparations for the trip began in earnest. John made a long list of what the twins were to take with them. He pored over the list, crossed items out, added new ones and crossed them off again.

"Don't forget to take your bathing suits," the Captain advised. "Odessa has beautiful beaches."

"Bathing suits," John scribbled at the bottom of the list.

Just as the last Russian lesson was taken, the passports arrived, stamped with Russian visas. "I want to caution you both about certain things," the Captain said, handing the passports to the twins. "Russian laws are severe. What we consider a minor breach of regulations, such as trespassing, they might consider a crime. So watch out when you're walking around. If you go anywhere alone, tell the Douglases where and when to expect you back. Don't let anyone talk you into selling them dollars, even if you are offered ten times the official value. If you don't make any friends, don't take it personally. The Russian government doesn't favor what they call 'associating with foreigners.' And, John, if you want to use your camera, first make sure there isn't a sign prohibiting photography. Use your common sense and I'm sure you will have a wonderful time."

The Captain left the room, and John said with a grin, "Remember how Granddad carried on when we first told him we wanted to go to Russia? Now he's as excited as we are about it."

"Winona thinks we shouldn't go."

"What?" John put the passports down. "Why? When did she say that?"

"Yesterday morning. I was helping her shell peas and suddenly, out of the blue, she told me, 'Don't you two go to Russia. Nothing good will come out of it.' I thought she was referring to all those stories in the newspapers, you know, about foreign tourists being accused of being spies and things like that. I asked her if she thought it might be dangerous for us, and she said, 'No, *you* are the danger.' "

"She's out of her mind," John said.

"Wait, that's not all. She took a pea and plunked it into a bowl of water. Then she told me to look."

"What did you see?"

"Nothing. What did you expect me to see? The pea made circles in the water. That was all. I begged Winona to explain what she meant, but she wouldn't. You know when she clams up there's no way to make her talk. I only hope she isn't going to say anything to grandfather and start him worrying."

"She won't, and he wouldn't pay attention anyway," John said. "Let's just hope the weather clears up. It's been raining for four days now."

"Suppose it doesn't clear up? Do you think our flight will be delayed?" Madge asked anxiously.

"I don't think so, unless it gets really rough. But if we do have a bumpy flight, are you going to be sick like the time grandfather took us to Canada?"

"I was only eleven then. I'm sure I outgrew it," Madge answered hopefully.

CHAPTER 7

FLIGHT TO ODESSA

THE weather cleared up and the flight was smooth, but Madge was sick anyway. "Some people are like that. They get sick the minute they set foot on a plane," a stewardess explained to John.

"I'm sorry," Madge murmured, pressing a tissue to her lips.

"Try to sleep," the stewardess said. "It will make the time go faster." But Madge could not sleep. She spent most of the night tossing in her seat and telling John in a faint whisper that she could *feel* the plane was tumbling down. She fell asleep toward morning and went on sleeping so soundly she did not even hear the loudspeaker announce they were about to land in Moscow.

It was only a short walk to change planes, but to Madge it seemed like a mile. Her head felt heavy, and her mouth was dry. She stumbled along at her brother's side, pressing her pocket-book to her chest. As soon as they had boarded, she went to sleep again while John tried to read a Russian book someone had left under the seat. The plane was about an hour away from Odessa, when Madge suddenly gave a start and clutched at her brother's arm.

"What's the matter?" John asked in surprise. "Had a bad dream?"

"Yes, I—I dreamed we were about to land in Odessa. Only it wasn't daylight. It was dark. I looked through the window and—suddenly I knew that something terrible would happen to us down there. I didn't know what it was—something frightening lurking in the darkness. You were scared too, so we decided not to get out. When the plane landed, we hid under the seats, but someone came and began to pull me out. I couldn't see who it was. I could only see two hands. It was awful." Madge shuddered and leaned back in her seat.

"It was only a dream, so forget it," John said.

"I know, but I can't help thinking about what Winona said about not going to Russia."

"Oh, what does she know? Don't let's think about it."

"You're right, I guess." Madge took a deep breath and settled back in her seat. "My stomach feels better," she said. "When are we supposed to land?"

"Twelve-fifteen, just in time for lunch. I hope the Douglases have something good for us to eat. I'm hungry."

"I wonder what Steve's wife is like," Madge said. "Well, we won't be in the way much. We have other things to do."

John looked unhappy. "Madge. We'll go to that address, but do you really believe that Marina's husband is still there? Ten to one we will be told he moved out years ago."

"You've said that before, but I don't believe it. There's a shortage of housing in Russia. Grandfather said so."

"Okay, let's not fight about it. Better look at what I found under the seat while you were sleeping." John reached behind his back and produced a thin paperback.

Madge looked at the title. *"Chekhov's Stories,"* she translated. " *'Razkas'* means a story or a tale, right?"

"Right. There are two stories in the book, one at the beginning and the other at the end, but in the middle there is something quite different." John lowered his voice and looked around. The third seat in their row was empty and the rest of the passengers didn't seem to be paying attention to them. He whispered, "It's a kind of survey of the political situation in Western Europe and in the United States. Strange, isn't it?"

"It sure is. How do you know it's a political survey?"

"I got a word here and there—enough to grasp what it's all about. Grandfather did say that Russian papers distort facts.

Maybe someone is trying to let the Russian people know how things really stand."

"It's a great idea," Madge said. "A person could read a book like this in public and nobody would know it isn't what it says on the cover. But how do you think the book got on the plane?"

"Someone smuggled it on, I guess."

"That's exciting!"

"We better leave it under the seat the way I found it," John said. They put the book back, but they went on talking in low voices until the stewardess announced that Odessa airport was in sight.

CHAPTER 8

THE DOUGLASES

"YOU'RE going to like Odessa," Steve Douglas said.

"It sure looks great," John answered. Madge did not speak. Her head was out of the car window. She was taking deep breaths of air that carried the salty tang of the Black Sea. The sky was an intense blue and the sun was hot. Flower vendors were on every corner and the smell of roses mingled with an odor of fried fish and something that smelled like all the spices mixed together. The voices coming from the crowded sidewalks were not all Russian. Madge caught snatches of French, English and another language which she could not understand but thought could be Greek.

Feeling dazed, Madge drew in her head. The three of them were squeezed together in the front seat of Steve's old Ford. "I was thinking of buying a new car," Steve remarked, "but then I decided to wait until we got back to the States."

"When are you planning to go back home?" John asked.

Steve frowned. "We were supposed to return in October, but my company will be signing another contract with the Russian government and that means another six months. Viola, my wife, is delighted."

"She must really like it here," Madge said.

Steve didn't answer until he had negotiated a busy crossing. Then he said soberly, "She likes the trimmings. I have a much higher salary than I would be getting in the States. We have a free apartment and we're able to afford a maid. But Viola basically distrusts Russians. As for myself, the only thing I object to is being under constant surveillance. I am not trying to suggest that we are surrounded by spies . . . but you'll see soon enough what I mean." Steve's sunburned face remained serious as he maneuvered the car past a giant truck carrying two rowboats.

Madge turned her head to read a street sign. "I like the names of Russian streets," she remarked. "Isn't there one called Uyutnaya?"

Steve looked surprised. "Uyutnaya? Yes—not too far from where we live. How do you know about it?"

"Oh, I've heard the name somewhere," Madge answered in an airy tone. "It means 'cozy,' I believe."

"It does," Steve said. He swung the car around a corner. "Speaking of street names," he said, "this is the Boulevard of the Red Army. Old-timers, in fact most people, call it by its former name—the French Boulevard. Viola and I used to live in a hotel with the rest of the foreigners who work in Odessa, but about two months ago the government decided it would be better for us and cheaper for them if they moved us into an apartment. So they remodeled an old house and we got an apartment on the second floor. Here we are." Steve stopped the car in front of a tall, narrow building built of yellow stone. It had deep-set windows and a blue semicircular panel of glass over the door. "Now watch," he whispered. "There, across the street."

On the opposite sidewalk, a man in a dark business suit seemed intent on watching a passing plane.

"The same man will be here for a couple of days," Steve whispered. "I bet he even knows about your coming. Then someone else will take his place. It annoys us, but we can't complain."

"It would bother me," John said, picking up the suitcases. "Can't you say something?"

"What could we possibly say—that someone is looking at our building? Here, let me help you." Steve took one of the suitcases and led the way into the house.

There was no lobby. A marble stairway with a blue runner and wrought-iron banisters began almost at the door. "No elevator, I'm afraid," Steve said. "But the stairway is not steep. Come on. Viola is probably cooking lunch."

When they reached the second floor, Steve produced a key and opened the door. "We're here," he called. "Come in, come in," he said to the twins and they entered a sparsely furnished room. A table held a vase of flowers, and beyond, glass doors opened onto a tiny balcony.

A door on the left opened and Viola Douglas came out. She was not as tall as Madge had imagined, but very slender, with shoulder-length blond hair framing a perfectly oval face. She shook hands with the twins and murmured a cordial greeting.

Steve said, grinning, "They've had a glimpse of Odessa from the car and they like it already. Madge even knows the names of the streets."

Viola seemed indifferent. "It's a nice clean town," she said. "Not a speck of garbage anywhere."

"Lunch ready?" Steve asked. "We're all starving."

"In about half an hour. I just put the soufflé in the oven. Would you take John to the den please, Steve, while I take Madge to the guest room? They have enough time before lunch to unpack."

An arch separated the living room from a much smaller dining room where a round table was laid with crystal and silver and starched white napkins.

Viola opened a door on the other side of the dining room. "That is our bedroom," she said, indicating a double door at the end of a corridor. "This is the den. The guest room is across from it." Madge stood on the threshold of the guest room. Pale blue curtains framed the two windows, translucent vases stood on a small table, and there were knickknacks everywhere.

"I simply must keep one room tidy," Viola said. "Steve is so careless with his pipe, and his blueprints are all over the apartment. I keep several of my wedding gifts here. Steve's mother gave me this handmade quilt. These vases are wedding gifts too. They are *very* fragile."

Everything in here is fragile, Madge thought grimly. "Shall I start unpacking?" she asked, turning to get the suitcase she had left just outside the door.

Viola became alarmed. "Yes, but please don't bring that dusty suitcase in here. You can unpack in the corridor, can't you?"

"Yes, sure," Madge murmured helplessly.

"I have cleared a space in here for your clothes," Viola said, throwing open the doors of a big wardrobe in a corner. "There are no closets in this house, nor anywhere else in Russia, it seems. The top drawer of the dresser is yours too. I use the other two drawers to store the things I buy in commission stores. They are what we would call 'thrift shops' in America. Only people don't donate things. They bring them to be sold and they get a certain percentage of the sale price. I bought some wonderful tablecloths, all hand-embroidered, bronze candlesticks, a lamp. Everything was simply beautiful and a real bargain."

While Viola talked about her purchases, Madge looked at the shallow top drawer of the dresser, wondering how she could possibly squeeze her underwear into such a small space. She was bracing herself to ask Viola for one more drawer, when there was a slight noise behind her. A small china figurine had slipped off a stand onto the rug.

"That stupid maid!" Viola exclaimed. "She always puts things too close to the edge." Running over, she picked up the statuette and began to examine it.

Madge decided to forget about another drawer and went into the hall to begin taking her things out of the suitcase. Someone called "Hi there!" and she saw her brother installing himself in the den opposite her. His suitcase was placed on a big black plastic sofa and he was stacking his belongings on the two lower shelves of a bookcase that were apparently cleared up for him.

His jacket was hanging on a portable clothes rack. It looked like a pretty good arrangement.

"How're you doing?" John asked.

Madge mumbled, "Fine." She picked up a few of her belongings and carried them into the guest room, trying not to step on the little fluffy rugs that floated like clouds on the polished floor. Viola was still busy with the figurine, but she turned around just in time to see Madge move a set of silver-backed brushes to make room for her own brush and comb.

"No, no!" Viola moaned, rushing over. "Don't you see that those brushes have to be just here, so they are reflected in the mirror." She glanced at Madge's face and said lamely, "Of course, you need a place for your own things. . . . Let's see." She moved a couple of perfume bottles and a china talcum box closer together. Relieved, Madge placed her brush and comb the best she could. "You can put your suitcase in the storage room after you have finished unpacking. It's next door to the den," Viola said. "I'll call as soon as lunch is ready," and she left the room.

At last the unpacking was done. Madge sat down gingerly on one of the small easy chairs to try to sort out her first impressions. On the one hand, she realized that it was not going to be easy to live in a room full of Viola's fragile belongings—or with Viola for that matter. On the other hand, being in Russia, even hearing the hum of voices from the street below, was exciting. On their way from the airport, Steve Douglas had mentioned several places they could visit and they all sounded fascinating.

"But all this doesn't really matter," Madge reminded herself sternly. "We did not come here to see the sights."

CHAPTER 9

NEW FRIENDS

JUST as Captain Sullivan had predicted, the twins' first few days in Odessa were filled with sight-seeing. Madge and John were fascinated by the Palace of Pioneers with its majestic colonnade, Morskoy Boulevard that offered a breathtaking view of the Black Sea, and the port where ships from all over the world were moored side by side.

All tanned, all seeming to be in a hurry, people filled the streets, gesturing and talking at the tops of their voices. As John said, "There is a continuous rush hour here." Civilians mingled with the military and sailors from foreign ships. Languages mingled too—Russian and Turkish, Greek and Italian, with snatches of French or German. It surprised the twins that so many people also spoke English, or at least had enough vocabulary to help them with directions.

One afternoon they were sitting in a park with Steve, who had taken a few days off to show them around, when a boy of about fourteen approached them. He asked in English if he could look at the paperback John had in his pocket.

"Oh, a detective story!" he exclaimed, leafing through it. John offered the book to him to keep, but the boy looked uneasy and, with a hasty "Thank you, no, thank you," walked away.

"If you really want him to have the book, leave it behind," Steve said as they rose to go. "Just toss it onto that bench as if you didn't need it anymore. Then see what happens."

John agreed and pretended to discard the book. After walking

31

some distance away, Steve said, "Now watch!" and the twins turned their heads. A group of teen-agers were passing the book back and forth and saying something about the author.

"They're taking it so seriously!" Madge exclaimed.

"They are kind of serious," John said. "You never see any roughhousing either."

"Russian youngsters are mature in many ways," Steve said, "and most of them are well-meaning and honest. But they have their bad element too. You'll see it."

He was right. As soon as the glow of new sights began to pale, John and Madge became aware of youngsters gathered in the doorways taking sips from bottles of vodka and smoking cigarette stubs picked up in the street. Once, a boy followed them begging for American cigarettes and became so insistent that Steve threatened to call the *milicija*, which the twins knew meant the police.

When Sunday came around, Steve announced that they were going to a matinee at the Puppet Theater. Viola was going to go too.

"I thought it would be kids' stuff but it was great," John told Madge when they got back to the apartment. "The way those puppets moved was so natural. I wish I could see the mechanics and—"

Madge was washing her hands at the kitchen sink because it was safer than using the bathroom full of Viola's jars and bottles. She turned around sharply. "Is that all you can think about?" she asked. "Don't you realize that we have been here five days and we haven't been able to do what we came here for?" She lowered her voice. "You know what I mean, don't you?"

John answered calmly. "Sure, I know, but we can talk about that later. The Douglases are in the living room having a snack and we are supposed to join them."

"Okay, I'm coming." Madge hastily dried her hands on the kitchen towel. "But remember that tomorrow we start."

John nodded. "Tomorrow will be good. Steve is going back to work and Viola will be at the hairdresser for a permanent."

"Fine! But now we have to think of a good excuse for going out by ourselves."

"Don't forget that we have to find out where Uyutnaya Street is," John said.

"We can't ask Steve outright," Madge said. "He might suspect something."

"You don't want the Douglases to know—"

Madge shook her head violently. "Of course not. We have to wait for an opportunity to ask without attracting attention."

Madge and John found both the opportunity and an excuse for going out almost immediately.

"Have you two made any plans for tomorrow?" Steve asked good-naturedly, passing a plate of cold cuts.

Madge looked at John, who answered, "We—er—we were thinking of going for a swim."

"Good idea," Steve said. "Go to Otrada Beach. It is the nearest and very easy to find. You cross the boulevard, turn into Yasnaya Street and follow it. In one place it makes a kind of curve that will lead you to Uyutnaya." He turned to Madge. "Didn't you say you've heard the name somewhere?"

Madge nodded, trying to contain her excitement. She sat quietly while Steve finished explaining the way to the beach.

"You won't be home for lunch then," Viola said. "I'll tell Hedwiga to prepare sandwiches for you to take along."

Madge started to speak, but John was already saying, "Thank you. That would be great."

"What made you say that?" Madge scolded him later. "Now we'll have to carry those sandwiches around with us." John was making up his bed on the sofa in the den.

"I can put the sandwiches in my briefcase," John said. "Besides . . . Well, we might end up at the beach after all. That Uyutnaya address dates back sixteen years. Better face facts and not work yourself into a frenzy."

"I am not working myself into anything," Madge retorted. "I am perfectly calm." She turned and went to her room.

But Madge felt far from calm the next morning when she and John were walking along Uyutnaya Street. "Is that the place?" she asked nervously as they approached a red brick house. It was separated from the street by high iron grillwork.

John looked at the number. "No, it's number 2 and we need 3. It must be that gray house across the street."

They crossed the street and stood in front of a three-storied gray stone building that looked like an apartment house. Three rows of windows were separated by some ornamental sculpture and on the left stone steps fanned out from the wide front door. Above the door was a small semicircular balcony.

The front door was unlocked. John pushed it open and they stepped into a small empty lobby. A marble stairway like the one in the Douglases' house made a sharp turn and vanished out of sight.

"We can't go from door to door," Madge whispered, suddenly shy. "What are we going to do?"

"You want?" a hesitant voice asked from behind them.

The twins whirled around. A boy of about twelve stood in the doorway, sunlight making a halo around his freckled face and reddish-blond hair. His round figure was clad in a T-shirt and shorts. Blue eyes stared at each twin in turn. "I help?" the boy offered. He stepped into the lobby and closed the door behind him.

"Yes, please!" Madge exclaimed eagerly. "We are looking for someone called Arapov. Do you know if he lives here?"

"Arapov?" the boy seemed to be thinking hard. "No, he don't . . . did . . ." He took a deep breath and enunciated carefully. "He . . . does not . . . live . . . in this . . . house."

"No?" Madge's voice quivered. "But he used to live here. How can we find out where he is?"

"What you say?" The boy blinked helplessly.

"Let me," John said to Madge. "Did Arapov live here before?" he asked, speaking slowly and distinctly. "Two, three, five years ago?"

The boy gave a big smile. "I understand. We ask *upravdom.*"

"Do you think he means the superintendent?" Madge whispered.

"How do I know?" John sounded impatient.

The front door opened again, revealing a thin, elderly man with a long black moustache. "Ah, Kolia!" he exclaimed. The boy immediately launched into an excited speech. He talked so rapidly that neither Madge nor her brother could follow.

"Amerikanci?" the upravdom asked suspiciously. He glanced in the twins' direction, said something briefly and closed the door.

"He say," Kolia translated, "he upravdom here eleven years, but no Arapov."

John muttered, "I knew this would happen," then said to the boy, "Well, we must be getting along. Thanks for your help."

Kolia touched John's sleeve and pointed upstairs. "We live there," he said. "My sister Ksenia speak English very good. You visit? Yes?"

"We really should go," John began, but when he saw the disappointment on Madge's face, he ended hurriedly, "All right, thank you, but just for a few minutes."

Kolia beamed and gestured to the twins to follow him up the stairs. "Arapov . . . He your friend?" he asked.

"He is our relative," John explained and the boy seemed satisfied. When they reached the second floor landing, they stopped in front of a door with several names on it. Kolia produced a key and unlocked the door. The twins followed him through a large entryway with stained wallpaper and along a dimly lit corridor.

After a few steps, Madge realized that this was not really a corridor, but one big room divided into sections by partitions that did not quite reach the ceiling. Behind the partitions she could hear voices, radio music, babies wailing and a strange hissing sound that she couldn't place.

Kolia noticed her puzzled expression and explained, "Primus. People make food."

John said, "I think it's some kind of stove you can cook on, but I have never seen one. It could be—" He never finished because suddenly there was the sound of angry women's voices from the end of the hall and something metal falling with a crash.

The twins started, but Kolia just said, "Kitchen," and opened a door on his right with a loud, "Ksenia, gosti!"

"He means guests," Madge whispered to her brother.

A girl with long blond braids worn in a crown around her head turned away from the potted plants she was watering and stared at the twins. "*Inostranci?*" she asked Kolia. There was uneasiness in her voice.

Strangers, Madge thought. Then she said to John, "She's afraid to have us in here. Perhaps we'd better leave." But John had already stepped forward.

"We are Americans," he said. "I'm John Sullivan and this is my sister Madge. Your brother suggested we say hello."

The girl looked reassured. Dimples appeared on her cheeks as she answered, "I am so glad. My name is Ksenia Bulanova." She spoke fluent English with a strong British accent. "Please sit down," she said.

Madge looked around. The room was fairly large and full of sunshine. On a table in front of the sofa a big dictionary lay open with a sheet of paper covered with notes.

Ksenia noticed Madge looking at the book. "I am reading Jack London's *White Fang,*" she explained. "It's our summer assignment. I have one more year at the secondary school. High school, I believe you call it. It is a fascinating book, but there are many words I have to look up in the dictionary."

"Are many students taking English at school?" John wanted to know.

"Practically everybody studies English nowadays," Ksenia

said. "My older brother Arkadi is . . . Please wait until I find the right word—*majoring* in English. He studies in Odessa University. When he has a test, we speak only English at home. You call it 'total immersion,' I believe."

"That's right," Madge said. "And that is exactly what we should be doing. I mean, speak Russian all the time. We live with an American family and their maid is Polish, so we get very little practice."

Ksenia looked surprised. "I was sure you were staying in a hotel. You mean you are all alone here, without your parents?"

"We live with our grandfather in the States," John told Ksenia. "He couldn't come with us, so he arranged for us to stay with friends of his."

Ksenia nodded. "I see. We are alone too this summer. Our parents are in the far north studying some weeds and other growth in the White Sea. They are both specialists in the sea lore. They won't be back until September."

"That sounds really interesting," Madge said. "Couldn't the three of you have gone to the north too?"

"No," Ksenia answered wistfully, "we couldn't. First, we would not have been allowed to join the group doing that special assignment, and second we would have had to pay for our tickets and there would have been other expenses. But let us talk about you. Kolia said you are looking for someone."

Kolia, who was perched on the windowsill, announced importantly, "They lost relative."

"Lost a relative? Where?"

"Kolia means that we are trying to find a relative of ours." Madge spoke slowly, choosing her words. "He is . . . er . . . in his forties and his last name is Arapov. His last address was Uyutnaya 3, but it dates back several years. He must have moved since. I wonder if there is any way of finding his present address."

"Yes, there is a way," Ksenia said. "In every town in Russia there is a special office which has the addresses for the entire population. When people move they are supposed to give their new address to that office. Don't you have an office like that in America?"

"No, we don't," Madge answered. "People leave their new address with the local post office, but it isn't revealed to anyone."

"I see." Ksenia looked as if she only half-believed what Madge was saying. "If you want I can go tomorrow and find out if your relative still lives in Odessa," she offered. "It will be easier for me because of the language. Arapov did you say? What's the first name?"

John said lamely, "I'm afraid we don't know his first name."

"This is really kind of you, Ksenia," Madge said. "How can we get in touch with you?"

Ksenia thought for a minute. "Please come again after tomorrow," she said at last. "I will give you the information and then we can all go to the beach for a picnic. Arkadi is going to be home too."

"Are you sure you want us to come here again?" John asked doubtfully. "I thought the Russian government didn't like people to have foreigners in their homes, and—"

Ksenia would not let him finish. "I know, but I don't care," she said, tilting back her head, "and I am sure that Arkadi would feel the same."

"Well, thanks again for your help. We'll see you on Wednesday." John got up. "Ready, Madge? We—"

A sudden shrill ringing interrupted him. Madge turned her head. It was coming from an alarm clock on a small shelf on the wall.

Ksenia murmured, "I must have set it wrong," and forced a smile.

Madge was staring at Kolia. She wondered why he seemed so upset. Sliding off the windowsill, he cast an anxious glance first at his sister, then at the twins, then back at his sister. Ksenia gave him a slight nod. "I go too," Kolia announced, turning toward the twins. "I have a—a—"

"An errand," Ksenia prompted, and she picked up a package tied in newspapers and handed it to him.

As the twins were leaving they heard loud voices again. "Why are those people screaming?" Madge asked. "Are they fighting over something?"

Ksenia smiled. "Yes, about whose turn it is to use the stove, or the kitchen table. This used to be a luxurious apartment building, with only one apartment per floor. Now it is what we call 'communal house.' Every floor is divided into rooms, just one or two for a family. Everybody shares the kitchen. Can you imagine what happens when several women all want to cook at the same time?"

Horrible, Madge thought as she and John followed Kolia out. They had just reached the stairway when Madge saw a boy with a big bag of groceries slowly coming up. At the sound of English being spoken, he turned his head and looked briefly at the twins through big round glasses. He then walked past rapidly and continued up to the third floor. Madge barely had time to catch sight of his pale, serious face and dark, closely cropped hair. "Do you know that boy?" she asked Kolia. "He seemed to understand English."

Kolia scowled. "He Victor Naumov. His father teach him. He big shoot in KGB, know all languages."

"What did you say?" John asked. "Big shoot? Oh, I see! You mean that boy's father is a big shot."

"Big shot, big shot," Kolia repeated to himself.

They came out of the building and Madge stopped. "We *could* go to the beach," she said to John, "but I'm not really in the mood. Let's go back to the apartment."

"Fine with me. Which way are you going, Kolia?"

For a second Kolia seemed to hesitate, then pointed in another direction. "That way," he said.

The twins left him and walked in silence for a couple of blocks. "We should have known that after sixteen years the same people wouldn't be living there," John said.

"Don't remind me." Madge changed the subject. "What does KGB stand for, do you know? Kolia said the boy's father worked there. Isn't it the Russian Secret Police?"

"Yes. I think the name means State Security Police in Russian. Look, there's Kolia."

Following her brother's gaze, Madge saw Kolia walking slowly along a narrow alley between two houses. Almost at the same time a young man, also carrying a parcel wrapped in newspapers, appeared at the opposite end of the alley.

It happened so fast, Madge was not sure she had actually seen it, but as Kolia and the man passed each other, their hands shot out and the parcels were exchanged. Then each continued on his way.

"How weird!" John exclaimed.

"What do you suppose was in those parcels?"

"It looked like books to me," John said. "I'm pretty sure of it."

Madge's eyes widened. "Books? John! Do you think they were like the book we found on the plane?"

"Could be." John sounded excited. "I read an article once about books that are prohibited in Russia. Ordinary books, like the Bible, for instance. You can't buy a Bible here."

Madge sighed. "I wish we could find out more about all this."

"It's not likely we will. By the way, do you think we should tell Steve about our meeting the Bulanovs?"

Madge started. "Oh, no! If we did we would have to explain why we went to Uyutnaya. Let's not say anything. All right?"

"All right. But come. We won't learn any more standing here all day."

CHAPTER 10

ARKADI

ON Tuesday it began to rain and on Wednesday it was still drizzling.

"No use going to the Bulanovs. We couldn't possibly go to the beach in this weather," John commented as he stood by the window in the den, trying to peer through the rain-streaked glass.

Madge had come out of her room. "Not go to the Bulanovs! We have to. I couldn't sleep most of the night wondering if Ksenia had found out something."

"Suppose she gives us the addresses of several Arapovs? Are we going to go to every one of them?"

"Of course. But then she might not have found out anything. It could happen." Madge bit her lip.

At breakfast Steve Douglas noticed a tired look on Madge's face and asked what was wrong.

"She's homesick," John improvised quickly.

"This weather certainly doesn't help matters," Steve said. "Let's hope it clears up, so that we can go sailing Sunday. Do you have any plans for today?"

John answered vaguely, "Oh, just wander around."

Steve nodded. "Why not? Lots of places you haven't seen yet. Museum of Arts, for instance. And don't hesitate to ask people for directions. Most of them will be happy to help, especially when they realize you're here for the first time."

Viola put down her coffee cup. "Asking directions is all

right," she said, "but please try to be careful. The minute people see American tourists, they try to start a conversation and the next thing you know they're asking you to get them a book that is prohibited, or to smuggle a letter over the border or something of that kind. Steve could lose his contract if he got mixed up in anything like that."

John blushed to the ears and Madge stared at her plate. Steve protested. "Oh, come on, Viola. It's not really that bad."

"Well, since Madge and John are going sight-seeing and I have a lot of errands to do, I better tell Hedwiga there will be no one at home for lunch."

"There is a lot of truth in what my wife was saying just now," Steve said. "But still don't think that every Russian who approaches you is likely to ask favors. Just have a good time. Better take your raincoats along. It seems to have let up but it might rain again."

It started to rain just as the twins were approaching Uyutnaya 3. Kolia waved to them from inside the front door. "Ksenia say you don't come. I say you come!" he shouted to them as they raced up the front steps.

Madge brushed the wet strands of hair off her face and saw that Kolia was not alone. A tall young man in a green sweatshirt held out his hand.

"How do you do?" he said. "I am Arkadi. The eldest of the family." He looked like an athlete, lean and wiry without a trace of his sister's and Kolia's chubbiness. Even his face was different, longer and thinner with high cheekbones. "It was nice of you to come in spite of the rain," he told the twins. "The beach is out, of course, but Ksenia has prepared a nice lunch for us to eat here."

"Do you know if your sister went to that address place?" Madge asked.

Arkadi smiled. "Ksenia had a lot of laundry to do, so I went instead. There are two Arapovs living in Odessa. I got their addresses. Actually, the minute Ksenia told me the name, I realized I knew a girl named Arapova. I mean, I know her by sight.

She is a student in Odessa University and quite a prominent member of Komsomol—that is the youth branch of the Communist party. Yes, I know you are looking for a man, but perhaps she could give you a lead. The other Arapov is a retired professor."

"Retired." Madge looked disappointed. "That's not him then. Our—er—relative would be younger. But we will go and see both those people tomorrow. Thank you so much."

"Glad to oblige," Arkadi answered.

Ksenia met them outside the apartment door. Her dress was covered by a big apron. "I am so glad you came," she said. "Come in. Lunch is all ready. All I have to do is to bring it from the kitchen." She giggled. "I was lucky today. The woman who is the biggest kitchen troublemaker is away, so I could cook in peace." Turning to her younger brother, she said, "Kolia, go and borrow a chair next door, please."

Soon everybody was seated around the table and Ksenia proudly served a big dish of *kotleti*, which Madge mentally compared to chopped steaks; only they were thinner and oval instead of round. There were fried potatoes to go with the kotleti and a green salad. Slices of watermelon that both John and Madge found much more sugary than in the States finished off the meal.

Ksenia and her brothers were easy to talk to because everything interested them. John described their grandfather and told how he had been all over the world on his freighter.

"What a wonderful life!" Arkadi exclaimed. "Do you know that Ksenia wanted to be a sailor once?"

Ksenia laughed and said, "Well, I was only ten and reading *Treasure Island*. I could have become a sailor though. We have women sailors and even women captains in Russia. But I have decided to study archaeology when I enter the university."

"It must be nice to have your mind made up already. I have no plans at all yet," Madge confessed. "What do you think you will do?" she asked Arkadi.

Arkadi laid down his fork and his face became serious. "I am going to try my hand at translations," he said slowly. "I mean I would like to translate foreign books into Russian. I would prefer writing my own, of course."

"And Kolia wants to be a truck driver," Ksenia said teasingly. Kolia was so absorbed in his watermelon that he could only mumble something in protest.

When the meal was over, Ksenia began to stack the dishes. "No, no, I can't let you go to our communal kitchen," she told Madge, who offered to help with the washing up. "I will be through quickly. Kolia is going to help me. Come, Kolia." Kolia got up unwillingly and, carrying his share of dishes, followed Ksenia out of the room.

As soon as the door was closed, Arkadi addressed the twins. "I want to explain something to you so that there is no misunderstanding," he said gravely. "Kolia thinks that you saw him last Monday in an alley about a block away from here. We don't want you to think he was doing something bad. He was simply exchanging books."

John started to say something, but Arkadi wouldn't let him. "Please let me finish," he said. "I want you to understand the situation. Most of us Russians are avid readers. Our interest in Western literature is immense, but a great part of the books published abroad, whether in Russian or in a foreign language, are not allowed here because they are not 'ideologically right.' Do you realize, for instance, that it is impossible to buy a Bible or get one from a library, unless one can prove it is needed in connection with one's study? Even then it is a long procedure to get a Bible out of the 'closed section.' For these past few years, some organizations abroad started to send books to Russia. I have no idea just how the books are smuggled in, but they are passed from hand to hand and no names are asked. All Kolia knows is that he has to be at such and such a place at a certain hour. He has no idea who the man was who exchanged books with him. It is safer this way, but please, *please* understand one thing"—Arkadi leaned across the table—"we simply want to know how things are in the Western world and we want to judge for ourselves as to what is right or wrong."

He paused and Madge exclaimed, "John and I found a book under the seat of the plane coming to Odessa. The title was *Chekhov's Stories,* but in the middle was—"

"Some political information," Arkadi finished for her. "Yes, I've heard about such books."

"I heard that Russian writers have all their books censored before they can be published. Is that true?" John asked.

Arkadi nodded. "Quite true. Every manuscript is censored by Glavlit and not every book passes their inspection. That is how Samizdat began. Let me show you what I mean." Rising from the table, Arkadi motioned to the twins to follow him. They entered a narrow slip of a room off the main living area, which seemed even smaller because most of the walls were taken by bookshelves. At one end was a bed and bedside table. At the other, by the window, stood a small table with a typewriter that had a neat stack of paper beside it.

"Ksenia sleeps in here," Arkadi explained. "But in the daytime she lets me have this room for my writing. Kolia and I share the bed in the living room. Our parents' room is over there." He nodded at a narrow door between the bookshelves. "It's very small, but at least they have some privacy. Look at the books," Arkadi said. "Go ahead."

John reached for one in orange paper covers and opened it. "It's typewritten!" he exclaimed, and Madge, who had taken another book, said almost at the same time, "This one is typewritten too!"

"They are all typewritten," Arkadi said. "Whenever an author writes something he knows will not be approved by the government, or if he fails to get the manuscript through Glavlit, he simply types as many carbon copies as he can, binds the manuscript somehow and lets it pass from hand to hand. It's called 'Samizdat,' a made-up word that's difficult to translate. You could say it means 'self-publishing.' Many books coming from abroad are duplicated in this way because there would simply not be enough copies to go around otherwise."

"Isn't it dangerous for you to have those books in here?" John asked.

"It is," Arkadi answered soberly, "but I know you won't betray us and I would like you to tell the story of Samizdat to your friends when you are back home."

The conversation was interrupted when Ksenia burst into the room with Kolia at her heels to announce that the dishes were all done and that the rain had stopped. "What about a movie?" she suggested. "There is a very good old one called *The Red Flower* playing in the local theater. It is a folktale. Arkadi and I saw it years ago, but Kolia has not seen it."

"It sounds great, but—" John looked at his sister—"we are supposed to be back for dinner around six."

"The first showing is at two-thirty. You will be back just in time. Do come," Arkadi said.

Madge hesitated. "I don't know whether we should or not. The Douglases, the people we are staying with, might think something has happened to us. Could I call them to say we might be late?"

"Of course," Ksenia said. "The telephone is in the corridor outside. Kolia, show Madge where the telephone is."

The telephone rang and rang, but there was no answer. Viola was probably out shopping and Hedwiga either did not hear or did not want to answer.

"Oh, well, why worry?" John said. "Arkadi thinks we'll be back in time."

The sun was just coming out when they left the building, but the streets were still wet. A dark-haired boy was standing on the top step, leaning against a stone pillar. He turned his head and Madge recognized Victor Naumov. There was a wistful look behind his thick glasses as he looked at the talking and laughing group going down the steps.

"Could we ask that boy, Victor, to come with us?" Madge whispered to Ksenia. The girl did not answer, but simply shook her head. Kolia said loudly, "We don't want him." Arkadi made no comment.

"What made you want him to join us?" John asked crossly when they were out of earshot.

"He looked so lonely," Madge explained. "I felt sorry for him. "You didn't want him along because of his father, right?" she asked Arkadi.

It was Kolia who answered first. "Because he *stukach.*"

"Oh, Kolia, don't say that!" Ksenia exclaimed. "We don't know for sure." Lowering her voice, she turned to Madge. "We suspect that Victor spies on the other tenants and reports to his father. His mother died two years ago."

Arkadi broke in, changing the subject. "What kind of movies do you like best, John?" John described his favorites and the conversation continued until they reached the theater.

The Red Flower turned out to be an enchanting film, but Madge found she could not concentrate. She kept fingering the slip of paper in her pocket with the two addresses Arkadi had gotten for her, thinking, tomorrow we shall find out. . . .

CHAPTER 11

TROUBLE

ARKADI was right. It was barely five-thirty when the twins entered the Douglases' apartment. Hedwiga, who had opened the door for them, mumbled something and shuffled away in her felt slippers. From the kitchen came delicious smells. Viola was probably adding something of her own to Hedwiga's cooking.

"Well, we made it on time," John remarked, taking off his raincoat.

Madge was unbuttoning hers when Viola suddenly appeared in front of them. "Where have you been?" she asked. Before either of the twins had time to answer, she went on. "Please don't try to invent excuses. I saw you with my own eyes entering a movie theater with some Russians. Where did they pick you up? What did they want from you? Jeans? Sport shirts? Prohibited books?"

"No!" Madge cried, bewildered. "They didn't ask us for anything. They—"

"Let me explain," John said, pushing Madge aside. "My sister is telling you the truth," he told Viola. "Those people never asked us for anything. We happened to meet them and found out they could speak English. They invited us to see *The Red Flower* with them and that's all. Madge tried to call and let you know we might be late, but no one answered the phone."

"We're sorry," Madge murmured.

"The point is not your coming in late," Viola said. "It's being involved with those Russians, especially after what I told you this morning." She was about to say something more, but Hedwiga called from the kitchen and she had to go.

Madge made a dash for her room, and John followed her. "Well," he said, closing the door behind him, "what are we going to do about this mess? Tell the Douglases how we happened to meet Ksenia and her brothers?"

"No! Once we start explaining we will have to tell about father, and then Steve might think it's his duty to write to grandfather and ask him if he knows what we're up to."

"You have a point. He might do just that," John said. "But there is sure to be a scene at dinner."

But no scene took place. Steve kept talking about his work and only after the dessert was served, said casually, "I understand that you two made friends with a Russian family. Where do they live?"

"Uyutnaya 3," Madge told him. "There are two brothers and a sister. The older brother is a student at the university. They're all very nice."

Steve raised his eyebrows. "Are those young people living alone? What about their parents?"

"They are scientists doing some research in the far north," John told him. "They won't be back until the fall."

"They live in a *very* small apartment," Madge joined in. "There are several tenants and only one kitchen for the entire floor. Isn't it terrible?"

Steve answered soberly, "It is indeed. Makes one appreciate things more. However, I am pretty sure your friends' family is on the list of those entitled to better living quarters. New apartment buildings *are* being erected, but I understand it takes months and even years for everyone to have a turn."

"One kitchen!" Viola said under her breath. "How can people live this way," but to Madge's relief she did not continue her campaign against making friends with Russians. After dinner everybody went to the living room to watch a tennis match on television and the Bulanovs were not mentioned again.

Later, when the twins parted at the door of Madge's room, John said, "So we're going to look up those two Arapovs tomorrow morning. Or shall we just try one at first?"

"Both," Madge answered firmly.

CHAPTER 12

THE TWO ARAPOVS

"JUST think, in a few minutes we might find out something about our father," Madge said looking at a street sign. "Only two more blocks."

John did not answer. He wiped his face. "Gosh, is it hot! Are you sure this is where the professor lives?"

Madge glanced at him. "Yes. Why? Is your leg bothering you?"

"Just a bit. Let's cross the street. There's more shade on the other side."

The twins watched a car swerve around a corner almost on two wheels. "Reckless drivers," John muttered.

After two more cars raced past, they crossed the street and Madge consulted the instructions Ksenia had scribbled for her. "Now we turn right, and then to the right again," she said.

Soon a quiet, dead-end street came into sight. Grass grew in the cracks in the sidewalk. The brick houses looked old. Professor Arapov's house had a green roof and a curious lock of engraved metal on the door. Madge suddenly stopped. "Suppose he speaks only Russian?" she whispered. "What shall we do?"

"Don't worry," John said. "You're always studying that Russian conversation book. I'm the one who's still at the 'Please give me a glass of water' stage."

"All right, here goes!" Madge said, and she pressed the bell.

For a long time no one answered, but at last a woman with white hair and a rather young face appeared. She held the door on a chain and examined Madge's blue denim skirt with interest. When she was finished with that, she concentrated on John's sweatshirt with its bold I LIKE TENNIS across the chest.

"Professor Arapov?" Madge asked.

The woman nodded and, taking the chain off, opened the door. As soon as the twins stepped inside, she burst into a long speech at such a fast tempo that Madge couldn't understand a word of what she was saying.

"Ask her to speak slower," John said.

"Govorite medleno," Madge began, but the woman already seemed to realize she was not understood and gestured to the twins to follow her.

They passed through a modestly furnished, old-fashioned living room and a small den that had rows of dusty books lining the walls. A glass door tinkled softly as the woman opened it, and the three of them walked into a diminutive garden, enclosed by the surrounding houses. There was a narrow bed of petunias, a potted oleander and an old gnarled pear tree. In the rippling shadows of the tree, a figure sat motionless in a deck chair. "That's him," Madge breathed, staring at an elderly man covered to the waist with a plaid blanket.

"Profesor govorit po angliski," the woman said, then shook her head and pointed at her forehead.

"He speaks English!" Madge exclaimed. "We're in luck!"

"Yes, but I think she's trying to tell us he's senile. There's no use, Madge."

But Madge was not listening to her brother. She bent over the man, asking gently, "Marina Arapova? Did you know her?"

The professor did not move. Without raising his head, he whispered, "Ne slishu."

"Leave him alone. He told you he can't hear," John said.

Still ignoring him, Madge repeated her question louder. This time the professor looked at her. His eyes went from Madge to John and back to Madge. With a visible effort, he pulled himself upright. "You are her children," he said. It was not a question, but a statement. He paused, then said, "Marina is dead, isn't she."

Madge faltered. "Yes, she died when we were born. We came here to try to find our father. Do you know anything about him?"

The professor didn't answer and turned to John instead. "You live in America?"

Tense, his voice unsteady, John managed to answer, "Yes, sir, but—"

"Go back." For a second it looked as if the professor was going to say something more. Then he began breathing heavily. The woman came forward quickly. She placed her hand on the professor's forehead and made him lie back.

"Perhaps we should leave now and try again some other time," John whispered to his sister.

"Hush, he is talking to us," Madge answered.

The professor was sitting up again. "I don't know your father," he said distinctly. "Go back to America."

Saying something soothing in Russian, the woman tucked a pillow behind the professor's head and covered him again with the plaid blanket. The old man's head moved restlessly on the pillow then became still.

"I think he's asleep," Madge whispered.

"Let's get out of here," John said.

But it was not easy to say good-bye and leave. As soon as they were back in the house, the woman burst into another long speech. Madge understood only part of it and John was completely lost. Still, they made out that the woman was a trained nurse who had been taking care of the professor for over five years. During that time he had had two strokes. He had his good days when he was quite rational and his bad days when he could not remember his last name. He did not have any relatives and very few people came to visit him. Those who came were mostly his old students. He used to teach Latin and Greek at the university. As far as the woman knew, he had never been married. And no, he had never mentioned anyone named Marina before.

"John, I think we're onto something!" Madge exclaimed as soon as they were away from the house. "He knew about Marina. Do you think he's her relative? Could we be his relatives?"

John nodded. "It could be. I suppose we shall never find out, though. The man is too sick to talk."

"He can talk. He said he thought Marina was dead."

"He said something else too—he doesn't know our father and he thinks we should go back to America."

"That goes together with what Winona told me. But we must come back here and see if we can make him tell us more about Marina."

John answered doubtfully, "I think we should try again, but let's wait a couple of days. If we press him too much, he might have another heart attack."

"All right, a couple of days," Madge agreed reluctantly. "What time is it?"

John looked at his watch. "Just a few minutes past ten."

"Good! There's still time for us to see that girl, Fima Arapova. But let's hurry or we will be late for lunch and then Viola will scream again."

"Can't we take a bus?"

"I'm sure we could, but we might get lost if we don't follow Ksenia's directions step by step."

"All right, then we'll walk."

"It's pretty far," Madge warned. "Look, if it's too much for your leg we can go tomorrow."

"I'll be all right," John said and he began to walk ahead. Madge hurried after him, wondering why she felt so strange— as if someone's eyes were on her back. She looked around. Nothing . . . Just people walking . . .

After losing their way twice, the twins finally reached the building where Fima Arapova was supposed to live. It was a huge building, with row upon row of windows. Taking a slip of paper out of her pocket, Madge read, "Apartment 1A. Do you think that means the ground floor?"

"We'll soon find out. Gosh, what a big place!" John stared with amazement at the giant antiseptically clean lobby with doors leading off it. Each door had a row of name cards pinned to it.

"Several people must live in each apartment," John said, peering at the cards. "Look, here it says 'Efimia Arapova—Ring twice.' "

"That must be her." Madge pressed the bell.

The door flew open almost immediately, revealing a short, thick-set girl in a bright blue cotton dress that looked too tight for her. She looked as if she were about to go out shopping. She had a pocketbook in one hand and a net bag in the other. From under a dark fringe of hair, her gray eyes stared out at Madge. "Ha!" the girl exclaimed as if she could not quite believe what she saw.

Madge was so disconcerted that instead of the carefully prepared Russian sentence, she blurted out in English, "Are you Fima Arapova? May we talk to you, please?"

The girl gasped and, turning her back to the twins, shouted, "Shura!"

There was a sound of hurrying steps and another girl appeared, thin and frail, with a serious face and black-rimmed glasses balanced on her nose. She too seemed surprised by the visitors. "Kto oni, Fima?" she asked, backing up a little.

"How do I know who they are?" Fima snapped back in Russian. "You find out."

"Oh, they are Americans. I see . . ." The thin girl faltered. "What your errand, please?" she asked in a prim little voice.

John answered promptly, "We are looking for a relative called Arapov. His wife's first name was Marina."

Shura began to translate, but Fima did not let her finish. "Tell them that I am not from here but from Ural," she declared. "I was brought up in *detdom,* and as far as I know, I have no relatives. If there are any Arapovs in Odessa, I am not interested in them. Now tell them to leave. I don't want other people in the building to think I associate with foreigners."

"We understand," Madge said. "Come, John." They barely had time to turn around before the door slammed behind them.

"What did she mean by *detdom?*" John wondered aloud when they were leaving the building. "An orphanage?"

"I guess so," Madge said. They walked in silence until Madge snapped, "Why are you constantly looking back?"

John gave one more look over his shoulder before he answered. "I have a feeling we're being followed."

"Really?" Madge looked around. The throng of people was moving past. She couldn't see anything suspicious. "I don't even care at this point," she mumbled. "Who would want to follow us anyway?"

John didn't argue. "It's probably my imagination," he said, but he did glance back once again before crossing the street.

CHAPTER 13

VICTOR

"WE just have to go back to the professor's house," Madge said half to herself.

John looked up from the list of Russian phrases he was trying to memorize. "Provided we hit one of his lucid days," he said.

"We should go to the Bulanovs this afternoon then."

"Do you mean for a visit? Or do you have something else in mind?"

"Both. We should thank them for those addresses, but also I want their advice. They might be able to give us some more clues."

Madge and John were in the living room alone. Steve was at work and Viola had just left with Hedwiga to buy groceries.

John was silent so Madge continued. "Well, what do you say? After lunch?"

"Okay, if you want to," he said finally, "but I think they've already helped us all they can."

But fate was against the visit. No one answered when Madge knocked at the Bulanovs' door. She tried the handle, but it was no use.

"Let's leave," John whispered. "We'll only attract attention."

"They might be back soon," Madge said hopefully.

"Let's wait outside the building then, not in the corridor."

They were crossing the landing when they came face to face with the boy Kolia called Victor. He peered at each twin in turn

57

through his thick glasses and said in English, "Bulanovs are not at home. Would you like to come to our apartment and wait for them?"

John hesitated, but Madge accepted the invitation eagerly. "Thank you. That would be great. John, it's better than standing on the sidewalk."

"Floor three," Victor announced, leading the way. When they reached the third floor landing, he produced a key. "Please come in. I am alone. Father is not in town." They entered the apartment and passed through a small hallway with a rack for coats and a big chest covered with an old carpet.

Madge looked around. They were in a big room that looked like a combination living and dining room. It was spacious, but the chairs and sofa were pushed against the walls and a big round table seemed to float in the middle of the room. There was not much light, perhaps because of the dark green walls and brown upholstery. Two flowery cushions on the sofa were the only specks of color.

"Our . . . How do you say it—houseworker? . . . likes it this way," Victor explained, gesturing toward the furniture. "She says it is easier to clean the floor."

"You mean *housekeeper*," Madge prompted. Victor nodded, "Yes, housekeeper. It was nicer when my mother lived. She cut pictures out of magazines and pinned them on the walls and she had all kinds of china things. Our housekeeper took everything away."

"You should have told your father. He would have made her give everything back," Madge said.

"I did tell him, but he said 'Let her take the junk.' " There was bitterness in Victor's tone.

Before Madge had time to say anything, he went on. "Mother had plants too, in pots. I tried to look after them, but they all died. I don't know why. I watered them every day."

"You need to have a green thumb to grow plants. Just watering is not enough sometimes," Madge said.

Victor looked interested. "Green thumb? Is that an American idiom? I must remember it."

"You must be a great reader." John nodded toward the big bookcase visible through a door at the other end of the room.

"Those belong to my father, but I have many too. Come and see." Victor ushered the twins into a small sunny room next to his father's. A bookcase and a writing desk were piled high with a stamp album and some exercise books. On the bedside table sat a big china bulldog in absurd pink and lilac hues with ferocious teeth and kind eyes. "This is my friend." Victor patted the bulldog. "Mother bought him just before she died. I shall never let that woman take *him*."

Madge realized he was talking about the housekeeper again and wondered how to change the subject. John did it for her by striding to the table and exclaiming, "Stamps! I collect them too. May I look at these?"

"Of course. I will show you the Cuban stamps father got for me."

Left to herself, Madge opened the bookcase to examine the contents. There were a few brand-new paperbacks in English, *The Old Man and the Sea, Moby Dick, White Fang* and a few others she had never read. But most of the books were old— published in England. *"Tom Brown's Schooldays,"* Madge read, *"Coral Island, The Boys of St. Timothy . . ."* She was surprised at the quality of paper, thick like cardboard, and the beautiful illustrations in color. Another shelf held old issues of *Chatterbox* and *Little Folks* magazines. Madge turned their pages expecting to see stories for small children but was surprised to see that they contained stories for older children and even young adults. She thought the name *Little Folks* must have put off lots of kids.

Looking at the books, Madge only half-listened to the conversation over the stamp album. Victor's English was more fluent and idiomatic than that of the Bulanovs. Both Ksenia and Arkadi spoke slowly, making obvious efforts to construct proper sentences. Victor spoke with more assurance, as if he were used to conversing in English. Madge asked him, "Where did you get these books? They are quite old, or were you born in the thirties?" She couldn't help teasing him.

Victor laughed. "My English teacher, Miss Talbot, gave them to me. She came every day for two hours. One day we would take walks and speak English, and one day we would learn grammar and read books. I was eight years old when she first came."

"It sounds like she was British. What brought her to Russia?" John asked.

"She came here to work for a company and stayed on. She told me the story once, but I don't remember it."

Madge closed the bookcase. "Well, she certainly did a good job teaching you. Is she still giving you lessons?"

"Oh, no. She went back to England last year."

"You must miss her," Madge said.

Victor made a face. "Yes, I liked her, but sometimes she . . . I can't remember the word . . . Ah, yes, she annoyed me because she always talked about her other students. Vania never made mistakes in spelling; Lisa never forgot her homework. Especially one student she talked about—Marina something. She was perfect; she did everything right."

Madge caught her breath. At the same time her eyes met John's. He raised his hand slightly as if cautioning her to be on her guard. Madge asked casually, "Marina? We have some friends in the States who used to know a person named that. I think they said she lived in Odessa. Did Miss Talbot tell you her last name?"

Victor shook his head. "No. I suppose she forgot. That girl was her student years and years ago. Do you want to see my new camera?"

"In a minute. Do you have Miss Talbot's address in England?" Madge asked. "I am sure our friends would like to know how it is going with Marina."

"Address?" Victor seemed shocked. "I don't have her address. My father does not like me to have ties abroad."

"Oh, I see." John had taken out a notebook and pen, which he now put back in his pocket.

"Her friend, Miss Kelly, probably knows where she is," Victor offered. "You can probably find Miss Kelly in Alexandrovski Park. She feeds birds there every morning. She used to teach English in a high school, but she's retired now."

"When does she feed the birds? Early in the morning?" Madge asked.

"Yes, before other people come in."

"What does she look like? Is it easy to recognize her?"

"I suppose so. She has hair cut like a man's, and she carries a basket of food for the birds. Now let me show you my camera." Victor turned to John, making it clear to Madge that he had had enough of the English governesses.

"I must be doing something wrong," Victor complained, bringing out several blurred snapshots. "Look. This is my room. I took the photograph in the daytime, yet it is all dark."

"You had the wrong exposure," John explained. He looked at another photograph. "This one isn't bad—a bit blurry, perhaps."

"That's a picture of my father coming out of the front door."

Madge was becoming impatient. She waited ten minutes, then said, "John, we must go."

"In a minute." John began to examine the snapshots again.

"Goodness, I thought we would never leave!" Madge exclaimed when they were on the landing.

John seemed to be deep in thought. "Shall we see if the Bulanovs are back by now?" he asked.

"No. I want to think about what Victor told us."

"Don't get too carried away," John said. "We don't know the last name of Miss Talbot's star pupil. It might have been a different Marina."

"It was mother. I feel sure of it. And if Miss Talbot liked her so much, she probably knows all about her. But first we have to find Miss Kelly."

"Victor says she gets to the park early. We have to find an excuse to skip breakfast."

"I'll think of one," Madge promised.

CHAPTER 14

MISS KELLY

THE excuse Madge found was that they wanted to do some bird watching in Alexandrovski Park. "It's almost true," she said, trying to convince her brother as they hurried along the French Boulevard. "We *are* going to Alexandrovski Park and we *will* be watching the birds while Miss Kelly feeds them."

John's only answer was "I can tell you one thing: We're both getting to be first-class liars."

"Here we are," Madge announced as they reached the park.

"We should have asked Victor exactly where to look for her."

They walked the entire length of the park, peeking into side avenues, but found no one who fit Miss Kelly's description. "She *must* be somewhere around," Madge insisted. "We'll just have to look harder."

"Maybe she stayed home this morning for some reason."

"Don't remind me." Madge's face darkened, then brightened again. "John! Look!" She was pointing at a small flock of sparrows flying above the trees. Another flock passed, heading in the same direction.

John smiled. "Oh, I see! Miss Kelly's friends are gathering."

Then the twins turned into a side avenue and stopped short. On a small grassy area surrounded by trees stood a stout woman with short gray hair. She had a basket over her arm and was throwing handfuls of seeds to the birds. From time to time, she looked up and whistled softly and more birds came.

John walked over to her. He introduced himself and Madge,

63

and started to explain why they were there, but Miss Kelly only looked confused. She listened, sharp gray eyes looking straight at John.

"Well," she said at last, "I'm not quite sure what this is all about. Let's sit down." Shaking the last seeds out of her basket, Miss Kelly led the way to a stone bench under an old acacia tree.

"You mean to say," she began, looking at each twin in turn, "you are interested in an old student of my late friend Jean Talbot?"

"*Late?*" Madge gasped. "You mean she is dead?"

The Englishwoman sighed. "My dear, I am so sorry. I thought you knew. Yes, Jean passed away three months ago. Her heart was never very strong, and of course there was her age—I am seventy-two and she was five years older. But—excuse me for asking—did you know her personally?"

Madge was too stunned to speak, so John replied, "No . . . No, we never met her, but we wanted to ask her about a student named Marina."

"Oh, Marina Arapova!" Miss Kelly exclaimed. "Yes, she was Jean's prize student. What did you want to know about her?"

"We would like to find her husband," Madge said quickly. "We think he is a relative of ours. Someone gave us addresses of two Arapovs in Odessa. We checked and he is not one of them."

"Miss Kelly raised her eyebrows. "But—why were you looking for an Arapov? That was Marina's maiden name."

"Her maiden name?" Madge shrank back. "Are you sure?"

"Of course I'm sure. Her father was the younger brother of Professor Arapov, quite a well-known scholar in those times. Poor Marina lost her parents when she was quite small. Her father was killed in the war, and her mother died soon after. It was Professor Arapov who brought her up. He still lives in Odessa. I could give you his address."

"We went to see him," John said. "He couldn't tell us much."

Miss Kelly nodded. "I understand. His—er—mental state is not what it used to be."

"You don't know who Marina married?" John asked.

Miss Kelly sighed. "I'm afraid not, and I'm pretty sure Jean didn't know either. After Marina graduated from high school her uncle sent her to Moscow University and Jean never saw her again."

"But didn't they correspond?" Madge asked. "Didn't they keep in touch?"

A sad smile appeared on Miss Kelly's face. "No, my dear. You see, giving private lessons is not like being a governess in a home. A governess becomes almost a member of the family and would naturally keep in touch. But a tutor never gets really close with students. Marina did write once or twice from Moscow. That was all. Later we heard that she came back from the university and kept house for her uncle. I believe it was only for a short while. Then she must have left Odessa for good." A blackbird came sauntering almost to Miss Kelly's feet. She smiled. "I'm afraid my winged friends are going to miss me. I'm leaving for England the day after tomorrow."

"Vacation?" John asked.

Miss Kelly's smile became wider. "Oh, no, I'm going back for good. My brother lost his wife and he wants me to live with him." She folded her hands in her lap and went on. "It's going to be strange to see England again. I've not been back for so many years. . . . Jean and I came here in 1930. Such adventurous young things we were. We found ourselves jobs as clerks with a British shipbuilding company that had just signed a contract with the Russian government. You see, we wanted to see the world and we were both too poor to travel. That's how we happened to land in Odessa. Only, a year later the company went bankrupt and the entire staff went back to England. But Jean and I stayed behind. It was depression time and we realized it would be hard to find work in England. So we applied for teaching positions in public schools. There were few people around who could teach English, so we were both hired. I stayed with my school until I reached pension age, but Jean left after ten years to give private lessons. I think she was happier that way. She never liked big classrooms." Miss Kelly rose. "And now it is time for me to go."

"The twins got up too, but before they had time to say good-bye, Miss Kelly exclaimed, "Oh, I've just remembered! There is someone who might help you find your relative. Years ago, before he became paralyzed, Professor Arapov used to hire a man to row him around in a boat. His heart has always been weak, so he could not row himself. That man is still around. I think that everybody in Odessa knows 'Matros Joe.'"

"Sailor Joe," Madge murmured. "Where does he live?"

Miss Kelly laughed. "My dear, he does not have a residence and no one knows his last name. He is a tramp, really, doing odd jobs in the port, but mostly dealing in the black market. American sailors bring cigarettes with them and supplies of pantyhose and jeans—anything that might be difficult to obtain here. Someone like Joe is very convenient for them. They sell him the goods for double the price, and he in turn sells them to people for triple the price. Of course, black marketeering is against the law, but Joe is not easy to catch. The local fishermen give him shelter, and since they are scattered all over the coast, the police cannot track him down."

"Is he English or American?" John asked.

Miss Kelly sat down again. "Neither—Russian. But he speaks English. From what I have heard, he jumped ship sometime in the twenties and lived in New York for several years. Odessa is his native town, so he came here for a visit just before the war. Apparently, he did or said something wrong, because he was accused of espionage and spent ten years in a hard labor camp in Siberia. After he was released, he returned to Odessa and chose to stay here instead of going back to the United States. I don't really know anything more, but he might be able to tell you something about Marina. He was working for her uncle around the time she came home from the university."

"But how can we find him if he has no address?" John asked doubtfully.

"You are bound to meet Joe sometime or other," Miss Kelly assured him. "He's always around cinemas, theaters, beaches, wherever there are crowds, selling foreign merchandise from under his coat, so to speak."

"So that's that," Madge remarked after Miss Kelly was gone. "We still haven't learned anything about mother, but we have another lead—Sailor Joe."

John frowned. "We better find him. He's our last chance. And we can't go on looking for an Arapov anymore."

"Yes, I know. But there's still the professor. We simply must see him again. It's three days since we've been in his house. Surely, that's enough time for him to recover."

"Why don't we have some breakfast back at the Douglases, then go see him?" John suggested.

"Oh, there's no sense in doing that. Let's just buy some ice cream from that vendor across the street and go directly."

"Fine with me."

"How are we going to find Sailor Joe?" Madge wondered out loud, as they were walking toward the exit. "There are so many movie theaters in Odessa."

CHAPTER 15

UNEXPECTED ENCOUNTER

THE twins were coming back to eat their ice cream in the park, when they saw Victor sitting on the bench in the main avenue. He waved to them and Madge waved back.

"Did you see Miss Kelly?" Victor asked, making room for them on the bench.

"We did," Madge answered, "but she didn't have Miss Talbot's address." It's not for us to tell Victor about his teacher's death, she thought. Who knows how he might take it. "Miss Kelly also told us she's leaving for England the day after tomorrow and she's not coming back," she went on quickly.

This piece of news did not seem to interest Victor. "I wish I could see England," he said, "and France, and other countries. Papa promised to take me to Finland, but he is always busy. Have you traveled much?"

"Not much," John admitted. "But we did visit Canada, Niagara Falls and Disneyland in Florida."

"You've been to *Disneyland?*" Victor was really excited this time.

Madge laughed. "You look as if we told you we went to the moon. Yes, it was great. We were only eleven then, but I remember every bit of it."

She began to tell Victor about Disneyland. He was fascinated, yet she noticed that from time to time he turned away from her to scan the avenue. Suddenly, he stiffened and his eyes narrowed. Following his gaze, Madge saw Kolia coming toward them, kicking a stone. He was carrying a package wrapped in newspapers and tied with string.

"Hello there, Kolia!" John called and the boy beamed. As he came closer and saw Victor, his face changed to a scowl.

"My, you look hot," Madge remarked, looking at the perspiration glistening on Kolia's forehead.

"Very hot," Kolia puffed. "This good, cold," he said, looking at the remains of the ice cream cone in John's hand.

"Come, I will buy you one," John offered, standing up. Victor was on his feet at the same moment. Madge thought she saw his elbow shoot out, but it was so quick she could not be sure. The next thing she knew Kolia's package was on the ground. The string had slipped off and a couple of books and a newspaper fell out.

Quickly kneeling to pick up the contents of the package, Kolia turned to Victor. "You heel!" he shouted. "You did this on purpose."

Victor threw back his head and clenched his hands into fists. "Liar!" he shouted back. "I never touched your package."

"You knocked it out of my hand," Kolia insisted.

"Shut up!" Victor hissed and he moved toward Kolia.

Madge looked at her brother, who was just standing there staring at Victor as if mesmerized. Madge suddenly rushed between the two boys shouting, "Stop it, both of you!"

Victor stopped advancing. "Who cares what you say," he mumbled in Kolia's direction and turned back toward the bench.

Kolia did not answer. He picked up the torn wrappings, stuffed them into his pocket, and tucked the books and the newspaper under his arm. He scampered away, but just before turning the corner, he stopped to shake his fist at Victor. Then he vanished out of sight.

Victor said something under his breath and glanced in Madge's direction. Meeting her accusing eyes, he blushed, took off his glasses, and polished them with his handkerchief. Then he put them on again. "Shall we all go home?" he asked John.

"We're going home, but not with you." John's voice cut like a knife.

"All right." Victor got up and began to walk toward the exit.

"I am glad you gave it to him," Madge said. "But we're not really going home. We're going to see the professor."

"We're going home."

Madge stared at him. "Why?"

"Just because."

"Give me one good reason why we're not going to the professor," Madge insisted angrily. "You're the one who suggested we see him this morning."

"I simply don't want to go anymore. Isn't that reason enough?"

"No." Madge was about to continue arguing, but they were already in the street and people were beginning to turn their heads. She followed her brother in grim silence.

As soon as they were back in the apartment, he asked to see the letter Madge had found in one of their mother's books.

"What do you want that for?" Madge asked suspiciously.

"I just noticed something. Come into the den." Puzzled, Madge watched as he began to scrutinize the postal mark with Steve's powerful magnifying glass. "Look," he said at last.

Madge read the date 1953. "So what?" she said.

"So what? Up until now we thought it was 1963. It proves Miss Kelly was right when she said Arapova was Marina's maiden name. She was no more than a child in 1953."

"We'll have to find out her married name."

"But how? Are you really counting on that Sailor Joe? Fat chance he'll remember any names after all these years. As for the professor, I wonder if he even remembers his own name."

Madge whispered, "Are you trying to tell me we should give up the whole idea of finding father?"

"Right."

"I won't. I just won't, and don't try to discourage me."

CHAPTER 16

VICTOR'S FATHER

"ALL right, so you followed them. Then what?" Leonid Ivanovitch Naumov spoke impatiently and shifted his plate so briskly that the silver clinked.

Victor was looking at his father across the dinner table. He mumbled, "They first went to a private house. A woman opened the door and let them in. The second place was a big building. I did get a peek into the lobby. A girl was yelling at them to go away."

"Did you mark down the addresses?"

"Of course I did. There they are."

"Where? Oh, I see." Leonid Ivanovitch picked up a scrap of paper propped against his water glass. "Well, I suppose I will have to get my assistant to check who lives at those addresses."

Victor perked up. "You think it is important then?"

"Look here." His father's voice sounded tired. "I asked you to trace the movements of the Bulanovs, not to spy on those two Americans. However, since you chose to do so, we might as well see if we can find out what they are up to. They are a bit too young for an international intrigue, though. Now, let's talk about those books you say the youngest Bulanov had in his possession."

Victor sighed. He was hungry after his long walk and the big dish of *komsa*—a small, tasty fish fried with potatoes and onions—looked tempting. "It's getting cold," he said, with a nod toward the food.

71

"What? All right, let's have dinner first." Leonid Ivanovitch heaped his son's plate, then took some himself.

Victor ate slowly, studying his father's face—clean-shaven, with sunken eyes, straight nose and high cheekbones. There seemed to be more and more silver threads in the dark hair, especially on the temples. For the first time he wondered how old his father was. About forty, he decided. Not really very old. Several of his classmates had fathers that age. They went to football matches with them or to the beach. Victor could not imagine his father going to the beach with him, but sometimes they played a game of chess in the evening. Usually, though, his father would go to his room and read or write until it was time to go to bed.

"Finished?" His father's voice cut Victor's thoughts. Victor nodded silently.

If his mother were still alive, Victor thought, there would be dessert now. Stewed peaches perhaps, looking nice and cool in a crystal bowl. He had never been close to his mother, yet when she died Victor had felt an emptiness around him that was still there.

Leonid Ivanovitch leaned back in his chair and lit a cigarette. "Now let's get to the more serious business. You said that the young Bulanov was carrying two books. Did you see the titles?"

"One was *Doctor Zhivago.*"

"That old thing! I thought everybody in Russia had read it by now. Not important. What about the other one?"

"I couldn't see the whole title, only the word *Red* and, I think, there was something about *Noon.*"

"*Red Square at Noon,* no doubt. That's more interesting. Were those real books or Samizdat? Do you know the difference?"

"Yes, Samizdat is usually typed. No, those were real books."

"Published abroad, naturally. Was there anything else in that package?"

"Some kind of newspaper. I couldn't see much because of the way it was folded."

Leonid Ivanovitch's eyes narrowed. "It must have been the *Chronicle*. That paper gives us more trouble than all the foreign propaganda put together."

"You mean the things they say in it are not true?"

His father did not seem to hear Victor's question. "Of course the Bulanov boy gets all that literature for his brother and sister. He is too young for it himself," he said pensively. "But he doesn't pick it from the trees. Someone gives it to him. But who? I'll bet you anything it is a different person every time. That's what makes it so difficult to catch those people. Try to talk to the boy. He might say something that would give us a clue."

Without raising his head, Victor answered, "It is no use to ask me to make Kolia talk, Papa. He wouldn't speak to me even if I paid him for it."

"I see. Forget it then." Leonid Ivanovitch got up and crushed his cigarette in an ashtray. "Need help with washing up?"

Victor shook his head. "No."

"Good. I have some work to do." Leonid Ivanovitch picked up the slip of paper with the two addresses, stuck it into his pocket and went to his room. Victor watched him sit down at his desk and unscrew his fountain pen. No chess then. Resigned, Victor picked up the two plates and silverware and went to the kitchen.

After washing up was done and the leftover fish had been stored in the refrigerator, Victor wondered what to do next. He could go out or stay home and read about the headless horseman in a book he had borrowed from the library. He decided to stay at home. Going to his room, he flung himself on the bed. From the bedside table the china bulldog watched him with big bulging eyes.

Victor's thoughts went back to his mother. How she hated those long, silent evenings. She would murmur something about needing fresh air, dress up, and disappear until late at night. She used to be a waitress until she got married, and she liked to visit with the girls who had worked with her. Reaching out, Victor patted the bulldog's pink and lilac head. Did those American kids have a dog, he wondered. He had hoped they would visit him again, but he knew they wouldn't now.

Victor turned over and began to pummel his pillow. Everything had turned out wrong somehow. He had not meant to spy on Madge and John the day he had followed them to those two addresses. He had simply happened to see them from a distance and thought he would join them. But then they turned into a small side street and he had become curious. Perhaps he should not have told his father about their strange doings. On the other hand, they deserved whatever they got. They had no business taking sides with Kolia. Installing himself more comfortably on the bed, Victor picked up his book and began to turn the worn-out pages.

CHAPTER 17

SAILOR JOE

FINDING Sailor Joe turned out to be more difficult than Madge thought. The twins walked up and down Morskoy Boulevard, along the streets where movie houses were located and up and down the beach, scanning the crowd for a man that fit Miss Kelly's description. John was not much help. He walked with a sulky expression on his face, muttered something about "looking for a needle in a haystack" and refused point-blank to ask for Kolia's help when Madge suggested it. "The boy is already involved in enough risky business with those books," he said. "Forget him."

"You were all for finding Sailor Joe and now you don't care," Madge told her brother. "But we're going to find him."

They did find him the very next day, in the middle of the morning. Madge had suggested they explore the area around the railway station, and they saw him almost at once. A thin figure with stooping shoulders stood leaning against a giant post hung with theater advertisements. Madge looked quickly at the sunburned face, gray mane of hair and gnarled hands and whispered, "He doesn't look like a Russian . . . but John, I think it's Sailor Joe."

At the sound of her voice, the man pushed a stray lock of hair away from his forehead. He thrust the tails of his red-striped shirt into his pants and gave her a long look.

"Americans?" he asked, switching his small brown eyes from Madge to John.

75

Madge answered him. "Yes, we are from New York. Are you Sailor Joe?"

The man grinned. "That's the name." He lowered his voice. "Got anything for me? A pair of jeans you want to get rid of? Nylons? Cigarettes?"

John answered from behind his sister's shoulder, "We are not selling anything."

"We only want to talk to you," Madge said. "It won't take much time."

"Hey, what's that all about?" Sailor Joe asked. The grin vanished from his face. "Look," he said, "you name your price, I name mine. Straight game. See?"

"No, no, it's not that." Madge laid her hand on the sailor's arm, afraid he might walk away. "We only want to ask you about that time you had a rowboat."

"Ah, that's what you want—to go rowing! Won't work. Sold my boat years ago. A good one it was." He shook his head. "Had bad luck all my life. Lived in America—worked in Brooklyn docks and made good money. Got married. But did I stay in America? No. Got it into my head to visit my country. Came here, to my own town. Went to the port to see the old haunts. How do I know new rules and regulations—don't go there, don't do that. Took a picture with my camera. 'You spy,' they say. Got ten years. Wife divorced me. Money gone . . . No point going back to America. Eh, what's the use of complaining—" He waved his hand and leaned against the post.

"But about your boat—the one you had," Madge said. "Do you remember the gentleman who used to go out with you?"

The sailor nodded. "Sure thing. A long time ago it was. A buddy of mine told me there was a gent looking for someone to row him around. Couldn't do it himself—had a leaky heart. So we got together and he hired me. Sometimes we fished, and sometimes I just rowed him to the Langeron Beach or some other place and we talked. A real nice gent he was. Then he got real sick and I . . . and I . . ." Sailor Joe's voice trailed off and Madge suddenly became aware that he was staring at something over her shoulder. She turned around and saw a boy of about fifteen or sixteen, suntanned and sinewy, in shorts and a T-shirt with an enormous mermaid splashed across the front.

Madge and John had seen the boy several times, hanging around the beach with a group of urchins. *"Hooligani,"* the other bathers called them. This boy seemed to be the ringleader. Now he was approaching Sailor Joe.

The boy's appearance seemed to scare the sailor. He drew his head into his shoulders and glanced around as if trying to escape. But the boy was too quick for him. He reached him in one stride and, without speaking, held out his hand, palm upward. This gesture seemed to scare Joe even more. " 'Scuse me," he muttered in the twins' direction and shuffled a few steps away, making signs to the boy to follow him.

"What's going on?" Madge asked John as they watched Sailor Joe and the boy waving their hands at each other.

"It looks like they were in some kind of a deal and our Joe did not come up with his share," John said.

Whatever the argument was about, Sailor Joe seemed to be getting the worst of it. He slapped his pockets, showed his empty hands to the boy and began arguing again. People passing by looked at the pair indifferently and walked on.

The boy must have been getting tired of bargaining because he turned around and whistled and four more boys appeared on the scene. Sailor Joe dove into his pocket once more. He produced a package wrapped in cellophane and offered it to him.

"What is it?" John whispered, and Madge whispered back, "Pantyhose, I think."

The offer seemed to pacify the boy. He stepped back and began to examine the package to make sure it had not been opened.

Suddenly, there was another whistle, but it sounded different this time. The boy hissed, "Milicija," and thrusting the package back into the sailor's hands dashed away. Sailor Joe stood for a moment as if paralyzed with fear. Then he streaked away with surprising agility and was lost in the stream of people. Madge was about to try to run after him, but John caught her arm in a hard grip and turned her around so that they faced the post. "Pretend to read the ads," he whispered fiercely. "The police might think we're in the black market too."

Behind them came sounds of whistles, heavy boots and shouts.

"Hello," a voice said and a hand touched Madge's shoulder.

"Arkadi!" John exclaimed and Madge whirled around. "That man—the sailor—did they catch him?" she asked breathlessly.

Arkadi looked surprised. "Sailor Joe? No, he escaped. He usually does. He knows the town like his own hand and has friends who are willing to help him."

Arkadi glanced around and lowered his voice. "In fact, he would have been sent out of Odessa a long time ago if the authorities did not depend on him for American sweatshirts and cigarettes. Sure he is jailed sometimes, but then he gets out and starts his business all over. He will lie low for a few weeks now, then reappear."

"A few weeks!" Madge was crestfallen. They were already in another street, moving homeward, when John nudged her. "Madge, Arkadi is speaking to you."

"Did you ever find that relative of yours?" Arkadi asked. "We rather hoped you two would drop in and tell us about it."

Madge made an effort to speak calmly. "We haven't found him yet. We're still trying."

"Madge wanted to see you, but I told her it might be awkward," John said.

"Yes, I know exactly what you mean. We should not associate with foreigners. But we still want you to visit. Please promise."

Arkadi's tone was so warm that Madge said impulsively, "Why don't you all come to visit *us?*"

Arkadi hesitated. "I suppose we could, but what about the people you live with?"

"It could be arranged."

"Well, we will see. Here's my corner. Keep in touch. Is that the right expression? We hope to see you soon." Arkadi waved and began to cross the French Boulevard.

"You should not have invited them," John said as soon as Arkadi was out of earshot. "The Douglases might not like it—especially Viola."

"I wasn't thinking," Madge admitted. "I'll talk to Steve first. He knows how to handle Viola."

John's answer was skeptical. "Does he? Well, it's worth a try."

CHAPTER 18

THE FIRST RIPPLES

"I can't bear it! It's too hot." Viola complained.

"It's only a heat wave," Steve said. "According to the forecast, we're going to have a strong wind from the sea that will cool the air."

"Oh, they've been expecting that wind for three days already," Viola answered. "Did you call about the air-conditioners?"

Steve looked unhappy. "Yes, but they won't be installed until August."

"That helps." Viola began to fan herself with a magazine.

They were sitting with the twins in the living room with the windows and door to the balcony wide open to create a draft. But no draft came. Prickly mist enveloped the buildings and trees and made the sky almost invisible. Even the refreshing smell of the sea that always seemed to be present had vanished.

Madge mopped her face and noticed with horror that the palms of her hands left marks on the beige upholstery of the armchair. Perhaps they would dry and disappear, she thought hopefully, folding her hands in her lap.

Steve shifted in his chair and remarked that his clothes were sticking to him.

"That's because you insist on wearing nylon shirts, and they are too hot for this weather," Viola answered. "Use your cotton ones."

Steve bristled. "My cotton shirts? No, thanks. With all the

starch Hedwiga pours on them they're hotter than any nylon."

He looked as if he were going to say something more, but he was interrupted by John. "I can't possibly send this. What a mess! The ink is running." He crumpled the envelope he had just addressed to a classmate and fell back in his chair.

Madge asked idly, "Why is the ink running?"

"Why?" John snapped. "Just look." He bent his head and big drops of perspiration fell off his forehead.

Madge giggled and John said, *"Very* funny!"

Viola rose. "It's nearly six. We're going to have cold cuts and a salad for dinner. It is too hot to cook and it's a nuisance not to have Hedwiga on Sundays. Let's have cold drinks first. Come and help me, Steve."

"May we help too?" John offered.

Steve waved him away. "No, no. Thanks. It will take only a few minutes."

"It's exasperating," Madge murmured as soon as she and her brother were alone.

"Don't talk about it all the time and you won't feel it so much," John said.

"I am not talking about the heat," Madge said. "I'm talking about Sailor Joe. If only we had had five more minutes, he could have told us everything. Don't you realize that he might have actually seen our father?"

Instead of answering, John suddenly asked, "Madge, how do you imagine our father?"

"How do I imagine him?" Madge thought for a moment. "I'd say he's very tall. He has fair hair. His face is strong and kind . . . and . . . and handsome."

"I see. But why do you imagine him like that? Don't you think there should be some resemblance between him and us?"

"Like what?"

"Well, we are not that tall and we both have dark hair."

"We take after mother. Grandfather told us she was dark and slender."

"But suppose . . . just suppose, he is quite different."

"I don't want to suppose anything. If only we could find Sailor Joe again! But Arkadi said he would remain in hiding for weeks. By the time he comes out of hiding we'll be home in the States."

"You're banking too much on Sailor Joe. For all we know he might never have seen Marina or her husband. What about your invitation to Arkadi, by the way? He must be waiting to hear from us."

"Who did you invite?" Viola asked.

Madge's heart sank. Viola was standing in the door with a tray of tall glasses. Steve was standing behind her.

"We . . . I mean *I* invited our Russian friends for tea," Madge stammered. "We had lunch once in their apartment, and I thought we should do something in return."

Ignoring Viola's frown, she chattered on. "I don't really mean *tea*. We could have soft drinks and sandwiches, and a cake. We would prepare everything and pay for the food ourselves."

Viola cut her short. "They are not to come here. I know exactly what would happen if they came. They would ask for some favor and that always means trouble. Steve's contract is ending in two months. If he has any trouble with the Russian authorities, it won't be renewed."

"But the Bulanovs aren't any trouble," Madge protested. "They—"

"They can't come here." Viola's tone was firm.

Steve brushed past his wife and put the tray on the low table by the sofa. "Freshly made lemonade for the young people," he announced. "Same lemonade but with gin in it for us oldsters. Now, about your Russian friends. I think Viola really means that it would not be safe for them to visit an American home. What about taking them to that fancy pastry shop in Deribassovskaya Street? The one with pink curtains on the windows and a big éclair over the door. There is a small fountain inside with tables around it."

"I suppose we could go there—" John began but Madge interrupted him. "A pastry shop is so impersonal."

Steve did not seem to have the strength to argue. Instead, he leaned back in his chair and closed his eyes.

A whiff of sea air came through the balcony door and died down almost immediately.

"Goodness, this drink was made less than five minutes ago, and it's warm already," Viola muttered, putting down her glass.

No one answered. Madge was sipping her lemonade, a deep furrow on her forehead. Suddenly, her face cleared and she announced cheerfully, "I think the pastry shop is a great idea! I'm going to call Ksenia right now and invite them all."

Steve looked relieved. "Good!"

Madge was making a beeline to the door when Steve called after her, "Where are you going? The telephone is right here." But she was already gone.

Viola made no comment except to say, "As long as those people don't come here."

Ten minutes later, Madge reappeared. "I called from the den," she explained. "I—mm—didn't want to bother you in here. Ksenia said they will be delighted to meet us at that place. She knows where it is. We are to meet them this coming Tuesday at three."

"Tuesday? Why not Monday, tomorrow?" John asked.

Madge hesitated. "Because—because I thought tomorrow might still be too hot."

Actually, she proved to be right. Even early the next morning the heat was oppressive. Steve departed for work, groaning, and Viola complained of a headache.

Right after lunch, Madge murmured something about having some things to do, and went to her room. John followed her.

"What do you want? I'm busy," she told him.

"What's eating you? I'm only looking for something to read. You brought a few paperbacks, didn't you?"

"They're over there, on the table." Madge pointed to a small pile near the window. John selected a book, and went to the den to settle himself in Steve's easy chair. In the next minute, he was fast asleep.

It was almost four when he woke up. His back felt wet and his head was heavy. A stroll might help, he thought drowsily, wondering why Madge did not come to wake him up. It was not like her to stay quietly in her room for almost three hours.

Stepping out of the den, John knocked at his sister's door. There was no answer. He peeked in. Madge wasn't in the room. The apartment was very quiet. Viola was apparently still nursing her headache. The living room was deserted. All he heard was the sound of running water coming from the kitchen. John decided to ask Hedwiga about Madge, but she only answered with a grunt and a gesture in the direction of the front door.

"She went out?" John asked. "When?"

Hedwiga lifted one finger and, turning her back to him, went on with her work.

Three hours! Where could she be? John let himself out of the apartment. Standing in front of the building, he scanned the street. Did Madge suddenly decide to visit the Bulanovs? Or go for a swim? But why make a secret about it? Why would she go alone?

In the next minute John saw his sister, walking slowly toward him. Her head was bent. As she came closer, he saw that her eyes were red and that she was breathing heavily. He called her and she stopped short. For a second they stood looking at each other. Then Madge whispered, "John, he's dead."

He stepped back. "Who?"

Madge burst into sobs. "Professor Arapov. He . . . He . . ."

"Wait. Let's get inside first." John guided her through the doorway and up the stairs. Once in the apartment, he took her into the den. "It's cooler in here," he said, settling her into a chair. "So you've been to the professor's. But why—"

"Why did I go alone?" Madge interrupted. "Remember that morning in Alexandrovski Park?" She was drying her eyes. "We were all set to go see the professor again, but you suddenly changed your mind. I reminded you the next day, but you said it was too hot. So I did it on my own, but—" Madge crossed the room to look down at the street. "It's all right," she said, returning to the sofa. "I just wanted to see if someone was watching the house." She looked at John. "We were being followed."

"We?"

"Ksenia was with me. But let me start at the beginning. I wanted Ksenia to come along because my Russian isn't that good. That's why I telephoned the Bulanovs from the den yesterday rather than from the living room. Ksenia met me in the street and we went straight to the professor's. Only we were too late. He was buried yesterday."

"Heart attack?"

"Yes, his third one, the nurse said."

"But what about being followed? You haven't told me yet," John urged.

Madge swallowed. "I'm coming to it. We were saying goodbye to the nurse when Ksenia whispered that there was a man watching us from across the street. I thought at first she was imagining it, but when we came out and started walking, he crossed the street and started following us."

"What did he look like?"

"I don't know. Just a middle-aged man in a dark suit. I have no idea whether he was a policeman or someone in the KGB. Actually, I was too upset about the professor to really care, but Ksenia was frantic. She dragged me through backyards, through buildings and down side streets and alleys, but the man was always behind us. Then we saw a big house that was being constructed. The workmen were busy doing the front, so we slipped in through a side entrance. It was really only a hole between two boards. Inside were just bare walls, like a shell. We ran up the stairway to about the fourth or fifth floor, I guess, and crouched on the landing. We stayed there for a good half hour. When we came down and got out of the building, the man was gone."

John looked stunned. "You were smart to hide in that building. I wonder what's going to happen the next time you and I go out. Is there going to be a spy behind us?"

"I wouldn't be surprised, but let me tell you something even more terrible. The day after you and I talked to the professor, two KGB men arrived at his house. They tried to interrogate him and the questions were all about us. They wanted to know what our reason was for being there. Had he ever met us before? Were we related to him? He wouldn't answer, and it took the nurse a long time to explain to them that his mind was not always clear. They finally left him alone, but they searched the house, ransacked everything, even tore up the pillows to see if anything was hidden inside."

"Did they find anything?"

"No. But toward the evening the professor started to talk to himself and to shake all over. That night he had another heart attack. He was very sick for a few days, then seemed to get a little better. Last Saturday he became worse again and died."

Madge looked away. "John, I feel as if we killed him."

John put his arm around her. "Don't. Professor Arapov was old and his heart was bad. He looked sick when we saw him. He would have—"

"Died soon anyway," Madge finished for him. "I realize that, but he might have lived longer if those KGB men had not come and upset him, and that *was* our fault. Remember what Winona told me? Now I know what she meant when she dropped a pea into a bowl of water. The pea made ripples and she told me we were going to make trouble for other people. She was right."

John winced. "Don't talk like that. You give me the creeps."

Madge nodded. "It *is* creepy. Winona knows things no one else does."

"Let's just hope she was wrong. Though, when you think about it, we could be making trouble for the Bulanovs as well."

"Oh, I forgot!" Madge exclaimed. "Ksenia said they are not coming to the pastry shop tomorrow. Not after what happened today. They don't want to be seen with us.

"Oh, there's another thing I didn't tell you. Just before the professor died, he said something strange to the nurse. He said, 'Marina wanted her children to be born out of Russia and now they are here. One of life's little jokes.' What do you think he meant?"

"What do you think?"

"I suppose she thought life would be easier for us in the States. I can't think of anything else."

John gave his sister a long look. "Well, if you can't, you can't. Why are you making such a face?"

"My feet hurt. I must have blisters on both heels after all that running."

"That's a good excuse for us to stay in the apartment for the next few days. Really, Madge, it will be safer for us not to go out. We only have a week left anyway, before going back to the States."

"We can't stay at home!" Madge said. "We have to look for Sailor Joe."

"Why don't we forget him and the whole business?"

"You mean give up our search?"

"That's right."

"But we can't! We've come this far. We just can't." Madge kicked off her shoes and limped out of the room, carrying them in her hand.

During the night the weather changed. Cool breezes blew from the sea and fresh air poured through every window.

CHAPTER 19

THE RIPPLES WIDEN

"IT had to happen just now—when I am about to start my last year at the university! Because two stupid kids decided to look for an Arapov. . . . Are you listening to me, Shura, or aren't you?"

Fima Arapova was pacing the room, her wood-soled sandals click-clacking against the uncarpeted floor—not that there was much room to pace between the two sofa-beds and long table piled with books and papers.

Shura, who was sitting on one of the sofas sewing buttons on a dress, looked up. "Yes, I am listening, but I don't really get what you are ranting about. Nothing bad has happened."

"Nothing bad?" Fima collapsed onto the nearest sofa and stretched her legs out in front of her. "I was called to the police to explain my 'relations with foreigners.' Isn't that enough? Relations indeed! I have never set eyes on those youngsters before. It gave me a shock when I saw them at the door. You remember the time I'm talking about, don't you?"

"I certainly do. The way you screamed 'Shura!' I thought you had visitors from Mars."

"Oh, *please*. It is easy for you to make jokes. You are not involved." Fima picked up a sheet of paper from the table and began to twist it nervously.

"Neither are you. Did you explain to the police that those kids were looking for an Arapov, but that had nothing to do with you?"

Fima gave her roommate a dark look. "No, I did not. Suppose they started looking for that Arapov and found him? What would happen if he turned out to be a dissident or something like that? And me with the same last name! I simply told the police that those Americans came here by mistake. As to my having nothing to do with all this, it is not always the best idea to insist too vehemently on one's innocence. It is wiser to give the police something to sink their teeth into, even if it has nothing to do with the matter at hand."

Shura put down her sewing. "It is getting too complicated for me."

"Well." Fima settled herself more comfortably and threw the crumpled sheet of paper onto the table. "The man who interrogated me asked if I knew a student by the name of Arkadi Bulanov."

Shura wrinkled her forehead. "Bulanov . . . Bulanov . . . I don't think I know him."

"You wouldn't. He is in philology, not science. I have never spoken to him, but I've heard rumors that he used to have gatherings of students at his home to talk about their plans for the future. 'Exchange of dreams' they called it."

Shura smiled. "Sounds innocent enough."

"That depends. It seems that later he organized gatherings of former students and asked them to talk about their achievements so he could write a book trying to prove that because everything in Russia is controlled by the government, there is no freedom to realize one's dreams. Why are you staring at me like that?"

Shura's eyes darkened behind her thick glasses. "Surely you did not tell all that to the police."

"Not in detail. I simply told them that Bulanov organized meetings at which anti-Soviet conversations took place. Later I heard that he did write such a book and that he intends to circulate it through Samizdat. Now say your piece. I can see from your expression that you are longing to."

"Oh, I am not going to say much." Shura jabbed the pin

cushion with her needle. "I only wonder whether you realize what a serious accusation you have made. The police have probably reported the whole matter to the KGB, and you don't even know if what you said is true."

"Is that all?" Fima asked sarcastically.

"Almost. I want to add only this: after what you have done, how can you look people in the face?"

Fima muttered, "I've told you already I had to divert the attention from myself. And now, if you don't mind, I have some reading to do."

She picked up a book while Shura returned to her sewing, and a heavy silence settled in the room.

CHAPTER 20

THE CHASE

MADGE spent most of Tuesday morning in her room. "I think I have a cold," she told Viola, who was looking at her suspiciously.

"It must be the change in the weather that got her," John said. "First that horrible heat and today the wind is almost cold. She just needs to rest."

"You aren't really sick, are you?" John asked Madge after Viola left.

Madge shook her head. "No, not really, only very tired and . . . discouraged. Suppose we never find Sailor Joe? We're leaving for home next Monday. There's so little time left."

"Just as well. We're only hurting other people at this point. I wish we'd never found that envelope. Madge, why don't we just enjoy the rest of our trip? There are still interesting places we haven't seen, and if we behave like ordinary tourists maybe no one will bother to follow us."

Madge didn't answer. "What do you expect to accomplish now anyway?" John asked.

"We could go to the professor's house again. The nurse must have gone through his things by now. Perhaps she found some letters or something that would give us another clue."

"Go there again!"

"All right, forget it. I'll go alone."

"I can't believe you want to go back there after what happened to you and Ksenia." John paused. "If I go with you, will you promise to give up this business?"

"No, I won't."

"Oh, all right. When do you want to go?"

"This afternoon."

John only nodded in reply.

But there was no question about going out that day. At noon, a gigantic thunderstorm swept over the town, followed by torrential rain that lasted for hours. Steve came home early because it was impossible to do any construction work on the pier. It was almost evening when the rain finally changed into a drizzle, then stopped altogether.

As soon as dinner was over, Madge looked at her brother. "Shall we go for a stroll? We've been inside all day."

"A walk will do you both good." Steve settled himself in an easy chair to watch a soccer match. "Don't go too far. It's going to be dark soon."

The streets were strewn with broken branches of trees and in several places lamps were out of order. A strong salty smell was coming from the direction of the sea. "I will miss Odessa," Madge murmured, breathing deeply.

John merely shrugged his shoulders and walked along with his hands in his pockets.

When they reached the professor's house there was a light on inside. "I'm glad she's still there," Madge said, pressing the doorbell. The nurse answered and let the twins in. She looked tired and did not seem to be particularly glad to have visitors.

Madge read a sentence she had composed on a scrap of paper asking if there were any papers they could look through, but the nurse was not helpful. There were no documents except the professor's diplomas and birth certificate. And there were no photographs. She was quite sure because the professor had left the house to her in his will and she had already done a lot of tidying up.

"Let's go," John whispered. "Can't you see that she wants to get rid of us?"

Madge looked around the den. The bookshelves were empty. The nurse caught her glance and explained that according to the professor's last wish all his books were donated to Odessa University.

"I thought we might look through those books and perhaps find a letter or some notes," Madge murmured regretfully.

John only repeated "Let's go," and rose.

Before letting them out, the nurse peeked through the half-opened door. "A drunken sailor keeps coming and begging me to let him pay his last respects to the professor," the twins understood her to say. "I explained to him over and over again that the professor was buried this past Monday, but he is too drunk to understand. He's gone now," she added.

"Sailor Joe!" Madge exclaimed. "It must have been Sailor Joe. We missed him."

John seemed not to hear her. He said good-bye to the nurse and, gripping his sister's arm, led her firmly along the street. "Why did you scream that way?" he asked irritably. "The nurse probably thought you were crazy. What did you expect to find out from that guy? Didn't you hear the nurse say he was drunk?"

"That's what she thinks. We don't really know he was drunk. He—" Madge suddenly stopped short—"John, there he is!"

The twins stared through the dusk. On the opposite sidewalk, a man in a striped shirt and old slacks was tottering along, his gray hair ruffled by the breeze from the sea.

"Come on," Madge urged, crossing the street. She wanted to call the sailor, but hesitated because she did not know his last name. Then she called, "Joe!"

The result was the opposite of what she had hoped for. Instead of stopping, Sailor Joe began to walk faster with unsteady but swift steps. In another moment, he turned a corner and became lost in the stream of people passing by.

Madge desperately scanned the crowd. It was a busy street and it seemed impossible to find Sailor Joe among so many faces. Still, she hurried on, almost dragging John after her. A movie theater came into view, and most of the crowd turned toward it. John stopped, but Madge pulled him along. "There!" she gasped. "I don't want to call. He might get scared again."

The striped shirt flashed across the street and vanished into a dark alley. Madge ran after it, but when she turned into the alley, it became clear that there was no more need to hurry. Sailor Joe was standing just a few steps away, his thin body shaking with a violent cough.

"My American friends," he exclaimed when he had recovered. "And I was running away! Thought cops were after me. Was risky my going out. Got to lie low, but someone said Professor Arapov died. Wanted to pay my respects. The woman there says he is buried."

"That's true," Madge said gently. "Remember the times you used to take the professor around in your rowboat?"

"Guess so." The sailor's voice was thick and his speech was slurred. "Guess so. A long time ago it was."

John whispered, "Let's leave him alone. He's drunk."

Madge brushed her brother aside. Coming closer, she asked, "Do you know if the professor had any relatives living with him?"

"Relatives?" A guarded look suddenly appeared on the man's face. "A niece was living with him at that time. Maria . . . Mariana . . . No, Marina—that was the name. Why you ask?"

"Because she is our mother," Madge answered.

"Eh?" The sailor's drunkenness seemed to disappear. With a rapid gesture he beckoned the twins into the shadows beside a building. They followed him silently.

"Must have a smoke," the sailor muttered. Reaching into his pocket, he took out a cigarette stub, struck a match and lighted it.

Then Madge asked him, "Did you know Marina? Tell us everything about her."

"Well, the fact is"—the sailor took the stub out of his mouth and spat on the ground—"I don't know nothing about her. Saw her only once—the night I smuggled her on that American ship."

"You what?" John exclaimed.

"Don't you shout," the sailor hissed. "It's a weird story, but it's true, so help me. One day, May 1963 it was, I take the professor out in my boat and he says to me that his niece got together with a wrong man and now she's expectin'. So he asked me to help get her out of Russia and get a fresh start. He says he got a letter from some friends in Philadelphia and they were willing to see after the girl, help her get on her feet. I look around and there is an American freighter ready to leave in a couple of days."

"The *Josephine?*" John asked and the sailor nodded.

"That's the one. The crew was all over town, you know . . . vodka . . . girls . . . He winked. "I got friendly with one of them, a young feller. Irish he was. Can't remember his name. He was about to get married and was willing to do anything for money. Professor give me some cash and we got the whole thing fixed. The Irishman promised to hide Marina in the hold and make her comfortable. He says he and a buddy he trusted would get her food and nobody else would know about her. In Hoboken they would put her on the right bus to Philadelphia. The ship was goin' into dry dock, so no stops for cargo."

"And then?" Madge asked.

Sailor Joe looked surprised. "Then nothin'. I take her to the pier at night. That was the dangerous part with guards everywhere. But we was lucky. The Irish feller and his buddy was on the lookout for us and took the girl with 'em."

"Was she very beautiful? Did you talk to her?" Madge asked.

The sailor shrugged his shoulders. "Never saw much of her. It was a stormy night and she was all wrapped up in a raincoat. She says thank you to me and that's about all."

John said softly, "She died soon after the freighter reached Hoboken."

The sailor nodded. "Guessed so from the way you were

talkin'. Only, we never knew. The professor was sure a letter would come soon. Instead his friends from Philadelphia wrote him letter. They says Marina never arrived. He was talkin' about tracin' the ship; only he had a stroke and I got arrested for selling American cigarettes. Got a year for black market."

"But when you got out of jail, you saw the professor again, right?" Madge asked hopefully.

But the sailor shook his head. "No. There was a woman, but not that one." He jerked his thumb in the direction of the professor's house. "She told me the professor lost his mind after the stroke. Now he is dead, and that girl—Marina—is dead. Eh . . . life—life . . ." He suddenly yawned and dropped his head on his chest.

In the darkness the walls loomed above them. The moon appeared between gathering clouds, and somewhere high above the roofs distant lightning flashed.

John said, "I think it's going to rain again." He held out his hand to the sailor. "Good-bye and thank you for telling us about our mother."

The man returned John's handshake limply. A drunken slur crept into his voice again as he asked, "You wouldn't have a couple of greenbacks on you, son? I sure could use a little money."

"I didn't bring any," Madge whispered to her brother.

"Never mind, I have a five-dollar bill," he whispered back. Taking it out of his wallet, he thrust it into the sailor's hand. "You might get in trouble for having American money," he warned.

The sailor retreated as if he were afraid that John might change his mind. "Was nice meetin' you," he muttered and disappeared into the darkness.

"Let's go back," John said when Sailor Joe was gone. "The Douglases will think we are lost."

Madge did not move. "John," she whispered with a catch in her voice, "do you realize that it's all over—we've found out who we are."

John's tone was strangely lighthearted. "We still have grandfather, and we don't have to look for our roots anymore. So everything is all right."

"Is it?" Madge whispered. "I wonder. . . ."

CHAPTER 21

A LETTER FROM KSENIA

THE next day Madge began to pack. "We might as well," she told John. "It's already Wednesday and I know Steve is planning something for our last weekend here. There isn't much time left."

"I guess you're right." John looked into Madge's opened suitcase. "Aren't you taking any souvenirs back home?"

"I was going to buy a few things, but I just don't feel like going shopping." Madge was throwing a blouse into the suitcase without folding it when Viola's voice came from the living room.

"John, Madge! There's a letter for you."

"Run and get it," Madge whispered hastily. "Viola doesn't know I brought my suitcase in here. If she finds out, she'll make me pack in the hall. Quick!"

John left the room, but he was back a minute later with an envelope in his hand. "I thought it might be from grandfather, but it's not—it's from someone in Russia," he said. "Funny, there's no return address."

Madge perked up. "A letter? For us? Open it."

Tearing the envelope, John took out a small sheet of paper and read the contents aloud.

"DEAR MADGE AND JOHN,

I have just realized you will be leaving this coming Monday. We cannot let you go without saying good-bye. Every-

98

thing seems to be all right. So please accept our invitation to a small party (just you and ourselves). I hope that Thursday night about six will be convenient for you. You do not have to answer, but we will be disappointed if you don't come.

AFFECTIONATELY . . .

"It must be *Ksenia* —the name begins with *K,*" John said. "The rest of the name is just a wiggle."

"Smart of her. This way no one could possibly know who the letter comes from. We're going, aren't we?"

"Of course. I would hate to leave without seeing the Bulanovs again. I suppose we have to tell the Douglases though."

"I suppose so," Madge agreed.

At five-thirty the following day, the twins set off for Uyutnaya Street carrying a small shopping bag with parting gifts. There was a pale blue nylon scarf for Ksenia that Madge had brought from home, and a hasty search among the paperbacks produced *Seven Days in May,* which they knew Arkadi wanted to read but could not get a copy of. For Kolia there was a box of chocolate candy.

Madge was worrying that Kolia would be disappointed that his gift was not American, but John assured her that he would gobble up the candy regardless of its origin.

They were entering the front door of number 3 when John happened to look back. "What's wrong?" Madge asked, seeing her brother's face change color.

He whispered, "I think we're being followed. There was a man behind us, but when he saw me looking at him, he stepped back. No, you can't see him now. Don't peek out. Let's wait a few seconds and see where he goes."

"Why would he let us see him?" Madge followed John into a corner of the hall where there was a view of the street.

"He didn't expect me to turn around, I guess. Actually, I don't know why I did. Instinct probably. Shhh, there he is!"

Madge watched with her heart beating furiously as a young man slowly passed by. He looked up as if to check the house number and then walked on.

"What shall we do?" Madge whispered. "We've led that man straight to the Bulanovs! We better not go upstairs."

"We can't very well stand here all night either—the Bulanovs are expecting us."

The twins climbed the stairs to the second floor, and saw Ksenia waving from the door and Kolia jumping around her. Madge forgot her fears and John seemed to relax too.

"I am so glad you could come," Ksenia said as she hugged Madge and held out her hand to John.

Laughing and talking, they went along the dim corridor toward the Bulanovs' apartment. Arkadi opened the door. He was smiling. Beyond him the round table was covered with a white tablecloth, with a big bouquet of roses in the middle. The door closed. The gifts were presented. The fun had begun. . . .

CHAPTER 22

DOWN THE FIRE ESCAPE

I T was almost nine and in Madge's opinion the Bulanovs' party was at its best moment. Supper was over and now all five of them were squeezed on the sofa. They had put the overhead light out and the big white moon seemed to float into the room. The phonograph was playing something pretty, but the music did not prevent anybody from talking. There was so much to talk about and so little time left for being together.

"What about your book? Couldn't you offer it to a publisher?" John asked Arkadi. "The worst that could happen would be for them to reject it. Then you could try another publisher."

"You don't understand," Arkadi said, leaning forward. "We don't have private publishers like you have in America. They are all part of the State. Not one of them would dare to publish my book, and even if it were accepted, it would never get past Glavlit. Not even a chocolate wrapper can be printed without their approval."

"But what could Glavlit have against your book?" Madge protested. "Ksenia said it's about a group of students who sit together and talk about their dreams for the future. I don't see anything wrong with that."

"Ah, but did Ksenia tell you about the second part in which I explain how many of those dreams end?" Arkadi asked. "Too often a scientist has no place and no equipment for his experiments because they are not of immediate interest to the State. A writer may be considered worthless unless he praises the heroes of industry. An abstract painter is a 'parasite.' Also, keep in mind that we have very little contact with foreign writers, scientists, poets or painters so there is no broad exchange of ideas. Everybody knows the situation, but only a few dare talk about it or protest. A book like mine would be called 'vicious slander' and could put me in jail."

"Samizdat is the only way for Arkadi," Ksenia said sadly.

"You mean you are going to Xerox your manuscript?" John began, but Arkadi interrupted him with laughter. "Dear American friends," he said, wiping his eyes, "please understand that owning a Xerox copier here is equivalent to owning a machine gun."

"We can take your manuscript to the States with us," Madge told Arkadi. "There must be a way to smuggle it through customs—our luggage wasn't examined much when we arrived."

"Give it to them!" Kolia cried, but Arkadi shook his head. "Thank you," he said. "I appreciate your wanting to help, but I can't let you do it."

"Because you consider us too young, just kids. Right?" Madge asked.

Arkadi smiled. "That is only a small part of my reason. Even if you were adults, I would hesitate. Authorities are dealing more and more drastically with people who smuggle manuscripts or art over the border. I don't want anyone to take a risk for me."

"We understand," John said.

"Aren't we getting too serious?" Ksenia suddenly exclaimed. "Does anyone want some more lemonade?"

They talked and laughed for another happy hour, jumping from subject to subject. Madge was just beginning to describe their housekeeper Winona, who could predict the weather, when running steps sounded in the corridor outside. The door suddenly flew open and a woman's pale face peeked in. "The KGB is here!" she hissed and the door slammed shut.

For a moment no one moved. Only Ksenia's hand found Madge's arm and held to it fast. Arkadi was the first to spring to action. "Kolia, turn on the light," he said and dashed into Ksenia's room. He immediately reappeared with a package wrapped in brown paper.

Running to the window he leaned way out. "No use," he said, straightening up again. "The ledge is too narrow."

Ksenia flew to her feet. "Arkadi! We can't let them find the manuscript. Perhaps one of us could slip out. Kolia!"

Kolia was by the door, cautiously peering out. He whispered, "No time. I can hear them."

"Give it to me." Madge took the manuscript from Arkadi and thrust it into her shoulder bag.

Ksenia cried, "Madge, you can't! Someone might see you."

Madge felt suddenly calm. "No one will see anything because we won't be here. Having foreigners would make it even worse for all of you."

John said, "Madge is right. We can try the back door. Quick!" He spoke calmly too, but Madge saw his hand shake as he turned the doorknob.

The long corridor was almost dark. From the direction of the front door came sounds of voices and steps. Behind them they could hear Arkadi telling Kolia to let him do the talking. Then the door closed and Madge realized with a shock that they had not even said good-bye to their friends. She almost turned back, but John pulled her arm and they tiptoed along, keeping close to the wall. A door opposite them opened and a man's frightened face looked out. In another moment, he withdrew his head and the door closed softly.

After a few more steps there was a bend in the corridor and they got a whiff of stale food and a slight draft as if from an open window.

"The kitchen," John whispered, pointing toward the dark opening at the end of the corridor. As they came closer, Madge realized that there was no door. It was probably removed to ease the traffic. Only bare hinges showed.

Madge saw a narrow door near the sink. "The back entrance," she breathed. "Oh, I hope it isn't locked."

They never found out because as soon as John touched the knob Madge pulled him back. "Someone is out there," she whispered. They listened to the heavy steps pacing the landing.

"Probably a guard," John decided. "We better—" He broke off and whispered, "Someone is coming."

Madge looked desperately around the kitchen. There was no place to hide. Yes, there was! In the shadows she saw a table made out of crates. John must have seen the crates too, for he was already heading toward them making frantic signs to Madge to follow. They barely had time to squeeze into the narrow space between the crates and the wall when they heard brisk steps and the naked overhead bulb suddenly blazed on, lighting up the room. A man's voice announced, "No one in here!"

Another voice asked, "Really? How strange. That tenant said he saw them going in the direction of the kitchen."

"Oh, well, the way you questioned him, he would say anything to oblige," the first voice grumbled. "The fact is they are not here and the back door is guarded. So they must have gone out some other way."

But the first speaker would not go away. He was prowling around the kitchen, brushing against the crates as he passed by. Madge tried to make herself as small as possible. As she moved, the wrapping paper around the manuscript rustled, and for a second her heart stopped beating. But the man did not seem to hear. With a curt "Let's go," he switched off the light and walked out, and the other man followed.

"Wait"—John stopped his sister as she tried to get up— "let's make sure they're gone."

When they crept out at last, Madge's knees were shaking so badly that she had to hold onto the sink. John went to the window and looked out. Following his gaze, Madge saw the rungs of the fire escape gleam in the moonlight.

"John," she murmured, "we can't go that way. It's too steep."

"Well, what do you suggest we do? Stay here?"

"Why not? Those KGB people are not likely to come in again and we could slip out after they're gone."

"Someone else is sure to come in. Perhaps the same man who told the KGB he saw us going toward the kitchen. You may be sure *he* won't try to cover up for us. No, we must get out."

Turning back to the window, John measured the distance with his eye. "The fire escape is only about a foot away," he said. "A long step would do it." He looked at Madge. "Come on. Let's try."

Grasping the window frame with one hand, he swung himself out onto the fire escape. "There!" he called softly and held out his hand to Madge. "Watch out now. Hold on till I tell you to let go. *Now!*"

Everything inside Madge seemed to turn over, but she swung her right foot out and leaped forward, trying not to look into the dark void below.

Step by step . . . rung by rung . . . It's only two floors, after all, she thought, but then she remembered the high ceilings. A dark window appeared and next to it a small narrow one—another kitchen and probably a bathroom. They were on the level of the first floor then. Madge began to count the rungs—one, two, three. She lost count and felt a jar when unexpectedly her left foot hit the ground.

"We did it," John said.

Madge looked around. They were on the south side of the house in a narrow alley that led to the backyard. At the end of the alley loomed the silhouette of tall gates.

John was peering through the darkness. "If those gates are locked, we could never climb over," he murmured under his breath.

"Perhaps they're just latched from inside," Madge suggested hopefully.

A blinding flash of light came so suddenly that John almost lost his balance. Madge caught his arm and they stood holding each other with their faces turned away.

A man's voice said in perfect English, "Please stay where you are." The beam from his flashlight swept across John's chest, lingered on his face, then passed on to Madge, making her close her eyes. Then the man shifted the flashlight, and for a minute his face came into view—thin, dark eyebrows and sunken eyes. The light caught the silvery threads on his temples and went out.

"Follow me, please," the man said. He turned toward the gates. A latch clicked and the gates opened slowly. "Please go straight to where you live," he said, stepping back.

It was only when they were in the street and the gates closed behind them that Madge realized they were free. "Oh, John!" she exclaimed, drawing a deep breath. "He must be a KGB man, but he let us go. Why?"

"How should I know?" John sounded irritated. "Let's hurry. It's getting late and the Douglases are probably worried."

Madge sighed. "Do you think we should tell them what happened?"

"I think we'd better. Let me do the talking, okay? Madge, I think that KGB man was Victor's father."

"Why do you say that?"

"I saw a photograph of him. Didn't you notice he looked like Victor somewhat?"

"Like Victor?"

"You don't notice things much, do you?"

Madge didn't answer. They were approaching the French Boulevard when she finally said, "What about Arkadi? Shouldn't we try to find out tomorrow whether he was arrested or not?"

"The best we can do for the Bulanovs is to leave them alone," John snapped. "Hurry—it's close to eleven." And they began to walk rapidly along the moonlit street.

CHAPTER 23

VIOLA INTERFERES

THE story John told the Douglases was somewhat vague, but he ended it by saying, "We were just leaving when the KGB men arrived, so they didn't see us."

Viola seemed upset, but Steve only said, "Well, as long as you weren't involved, there's no harm done."

Leaning against the wall with her eyes half-closed, Madge thought, But we *are* involved. If the Douglases only knew about the manuscript in my bag. . . . Suppose, suppose. . . She tried to hide a yawn behind her hand and promptly yawned again. Viola noticed her drowsiness and suggested that everybody go to bed.

Safe in her room, Madge pulled the manuscript out of her bag. Now, where to hide it? There seemed to be only one good place. Kneeling down, she pulled out the bottom drawer of the dresser and slipped the manuscript under Viola's hand-embroidered tablecloths.

Madge nearly fell asleep while undressing, yet when she finally got into bed she found she could not sleep. Had Arkadi been arrested? Were Ksenia and Kolia okay? Would it be safe to call the apartment on the telephone? . . . Then the nightmare began. Madge was on the fire escape again, but this time she was climbing up, not down. Below her John was calling, "Madge, come back. Come back!" She wanted to descend, but her feet were carrying her farther and farther up toward the roof. . . .

Suddenly she woke up. The room was flooded with sunshine

and behind the door John was calling, "Wake up, Madge. Wake up."

"Why? What happened?"

"I'll tell you when you're dressed," he answered.

Madge felt her throat tighten. "Give me a minute," she mumbled.

"I'll be in the den," he called and Madge heard him walk away. She pulled on a sundress and darted to the bathroom to splash cold water on her face. Then, smoothing her hair with her hands, she went into the den.

John was perched on a corner of the desk. "Steve was summoned to the police headquarters this morning," he said. "They questioned him about us."

"Steve?" Madge caught her breath. "About us? But what did they want to know?"

"What was the reason for our coming to Odessa? Were we related to him or Viola? How long have we known the Bulanovs? Did we visit them frequently? That kind of thing."

"Did they ask anything about the professor?"

"No. They seemed to be interested mainly in our connections with the Bulanovs. Steve explained to them that we met by chance and became friends because there are no Americans our own age in the building."

"Is Steve home now?"

"No. He was in his office when the police called. They only kept him for about half an hour. As soon as he got back he called Viola. Only I happened to answer the phone and he told me the whole story. He was very calm about it. Said it was probably a routine check and not to worry. But then he asked me to put Viola on, and when she heard what happened she hit the ceiling."

"I bet she did. What do we do now?"

John lowered his voice. "The best thing for us would be to clear out until Steve comes home. If you could skip breakfast, we might try spending the day at the beach."

Madge sighed with relief. "Fine with me. Let's leave now."

Hedwiga scowled at the request for a picnic lunch but finally slapped together two cheese sandwiches and added a couple of pears. Madge gulped down some milk while John composed a note to Viola, who was in her room. "I simply said that we are going to spend the day on the beach," he explained. "This way she won't think we ran away." He laughed as he handed the note to Hedwiga. "Not that she would mind."

The way to the beach led through Uyutnaya, and Madge looked anxiously up at the Bulanovs' windows. The curtains were down even though it was almost noon. She turned her head for another glance and saw Victor leaning out of a third floor window.

"John!" Madge exclaimed. "Look! There's Victor peeking at us."

"So what?" John suddenly shouted. "Let him look. Stop bothering me with that fellow, will you? Who cares what he's doing."

Madge was going to argue, but John looked so tense that she thought it would be better to keep quiet. Walking slowly, she tried to figure out what had provoked such an outburst. Neither of them said a word until they arrived at the beach.

"Shall we go for a swim or sit in the sun first?" John asked.

"Go for a swim," Madge answered. "I didn't even have time for a shower this morning."

The beach was not very crowded. The twins found a quiet spot and changed out of sight.

Madge felt refreshed after her swim, but John remained in his dark mood and grumbled about forgetting to bring a book or a magazine with him. Lying flat on the sand, he muttered, "How I wish we were out of here."

Madge turned over and looked her brother straight in the eyes. "John, what's wrong with you?"

"Nothing. I'm just tired of all these troubles. Winona was right. We *are* making ripples."

Madge said slowly, "You know, I've been thinking. Something happened to you that day we met Victor and Kolia in the park. You never even tried to stop the boys when they started to fight. And you refused to go see the professor after telling me just minutes before that we *should* go."

John's mouth tightened. "Nothing happened to me. Just leave me alone."

"Look, John—" Madge began, but he interrupted her.

"Let's have a nice quiet day here and enjoy the sea. Shall we?"

"All right," she murmured.

They went for another swim, ate their sandwiches and bought lemonade from a vendor. Around them the beach was becoming more and more crowded, and at five John suggested they go back to the apartment. "Steve will be home by the time we arrive," he told Madge, "and that's better than facing Viola by ourselves."

But when they entered the apartment Steve was not there.

Madge whispered anxiously, "Suppose she throws us out?"

John shook his head and pointed at the small table in the living room that held a tray with a pitcher of martinis, a bottle of soda and four glasses.

Madge was about to make a dash for her room to change when Viola came out of the kitchen. "Have a good swim?" she asked. "You're just in time for dinner." Before either of the twins had time to say a word, she went on, "By the way one of your friends called and asked to have back the manuscript I happened to find in my drawer, so naturally I gave it to him."

Madge was speechless.

"Who asked for it back?" John asked. "Arkadi?"

Viola shrugged her shoulders. "I don't know what his name was. He said he was a friend of yours, and he asked for the manuscript as if he knew all about it."

"But what did he look like? Was he tall?"

Viola raised her eyebrows. "Tall? No. It was a boy."

"Oh, Kolia!" Madge said. "Sort of chubby, with a round face. Reddish hair."

Viola looked uneasy. "No, no. He was dark-haired and wore glasses."

There was a minute of silence, then Madge exclaimed, "It was Victor! How could you give the manuscript to him? His father is in the KGB. How could you?"

"Don't talk to me like that. You two have made enough trouble all around and now *I* am to blame?"

Suddenly Steve appeared in the hall. "What's going on?" he demanded, looking around.

Madge suddenly burst into tears. Steve listened patiently as she explained how they had saved Arkadi's book and how Viola had delivered it almost into the hands of the KGB.

When she finished, Steve said, "My wife meant no harm. I am only sorry you didn't give me the manuscript to take care of. Anyway, the damage is done."

Viola flared up. "You'll be glad enough that I got rid of that incriminating thing when the KGB comes to search this apartment."

"No one is coming to search the apartment," Steve answered, "and now may I suggest that we all calm down and have some dinner."

The meal was not a pleasant one. Steve was trying hard to create conversation, while Viola kept quiet. Madge was constantly wiping her eyes, and John spoke as little as possible.

The minute that dinner was over Madge excused herself and dashed out of the dining room. "I better go see what the matter is," John told Steve apologetically as he left the table.

"I have an idea," Madge burst out as soon as she and John were safely inside the den. "We have to go to Victor's and make him give the manuscript back to us."

"That's crazy. His father is probably at home."

"So? He let us go last night. Maybe he'll help us again."

Sitting down, John began to scratch the blotter on the desk with his fingernail. "I'm not going," he said without looking up.

"So stay."

John half-rose from his seat. "You can't go!"

"You can't stop me."

"Madge, listen." John grabbed her wrist. "I want to tell you something." Then he stopped. "Never mind, let's go."

When they reached the hall, Steve came out of the living room. "Where are you two off to?" he asked, looking from Madge to John.

John mumbled, "Going for a short walk."

"Is that all?" Steve's gaze became hard and suspicious. "Look, kids," he said, "you assured us you don't have anything to do with the trouble your friends are having with the KGB. Is that so? Or is there something else going on you don't want us to know about?"

John blushed to the ears, glanced at his sister and blurted out, "Yes, we have problems of our own. It's—it's—something to do with our family."

Steve seemed to relax. "Well, I don't want to interfere. But if there's anything else that bothers you, please consult me."

"He would never have let us off so easily if we weren't leaving soon," John remarked when they were finally in the street. "He feels responsible for us while we're here, but in a few days—"

Madge cut him short. "I don't care what Steve or anyone else thinks. All I want is to get that manuscript back."

CHAPTER 24

FACE TO FACE

THERE was a light in the window Victor had been peering from that very morning. "He's at home," Madge said.

"*They're* at home," John corrected her. "Sure you want to go through with this?"

"Yes," Madge said and she began to mount the stairway.

As the twins reached the door to the third floor, a woman walked out with a bulldog on a leash. "Who do you want?" she asked in Russian.

Madge answered, "Naumov." The woman said nothing but stepped aside to let the twins in. It was obvious that she would have liked to stay and see where they went, but the dog pulled and she had to go.

Victor's father opened the door. A startled look passed over his face and Madge's heart sank a little. She stammered, "M-may we talk to you, please?"

Naumov answered, "Certainly. Please come in."

Madge recognized the hallway with its rack for coats and large chest covered with an old rug. When she and John stepped into the vast living room, she saw that the table in the middle of the floor had been set for a meal. Two plates were placed exactly opposite each other, with knives and forks and filled water glasses. A small vase with a green branch added a touch of festivity. Beside one of the plates lay a square package wrapped in brown paper. Madge recognized Arkadi's manuscript instantly and moved toward it.

"Don't touch it." Victor had suddenly appeared in front of Madge, barring her way. "You have no right to it."

"*You* have no right to it!" Madge said. "You came to the Douglases' apartment pretending you were Kolia. You stole it!"

Victor threw back his head. "No! I requisitioned it."

"Just a moment, please." Naumov went over to the table and picked up the package. "I just came home," he said, turning to Madge. "I am afraid I don't understand what is going on."

"It's Arkadi Bulanov's book." Victor laid his hand on the package as if afraid Madge might take it away by force. "You looked so upset, Papa, when you came home last night and said that our men searched the apartment and only found a few Samizdat books. I got it for you. Aren't you pleased?"

Madge saw tears spring into Victor's eyes. He snatched off his glasses and began to rub them with a corner of the tablecloth. He looks different without them, she thought. He looks more like his father now and . . . and . . . a little like John. Instinctively, she glanced first at her brother, then at Naumov, who was standing with his hand on the back of a chair. For a second the three faces merged, became blurred, then swam into focus again. Madge heard her own voice saying very quietly, "You are Marina's husband."

Naumov looked at her. The light from the overhead lamp caught the silver on his temples, making them even whiter. "Yes, I am Marina's husband," he began. Madge remained silent, so he went on. "We first met when we were children. She lived with her uncle, and since my family lived in the same building we often played together. Later, Professor Arapov obtained the house his parents had owned before the revolution and he and Marina moved away. We lost sight of each other. It was 1959 when we met again. I was sent to Moscow to investigate an unrest at the university. I happened to see Marina there. We . . . well, we fell in love and got married as soon as she graduated from the university. I must add that this was against her uncle's wishes."

In spite of herself, Madge asked, "But didn't she know—" and stopped because she could not find the right words.

Naumov understood the unfinished question. "She knew for whom I worked, of course, but she didn't know all. Later, she found out and realized she couldn't live with someone who sends people to concentration camps, prison or mental hospitals, because they dare to write or say what other people may only think. One day I came back from a business trip and found her gone. She was pregnant. I knew she could not have arranged to leave without someone helping her. That someone was obviously her uncle. I stormed his house, but he assured me he had no idea of her whereabouts. Soon after he had a stroke and that put an end to my hopes of obtaining any information from him. I left him alone—until the day Victor mentioned he had followed you two to a certain house. The address sounded familiar and then I remembered that was where Professor Arapov lived."

At the mention of his name, Victor suddenly cried, "But then you married Mama and everything was all right again. Wasn't it, Papa?"

"All right again?" Leonid Ivanovitch smiled for the first time. "No, son. Nothing became all right again. Your mother and I were not destined for each other. Your mother wanted to socialize, but my co-workers ignored her and people in the building would have nothing to do with the wife of 'that KGBist.' It was not a happy life for either of us."

Victor looked stunned. Naumov walked over and put his arm around the boy's shoulders. "I wonder if you realize these Americans are your stepbrother and stepsister."

"Yes, Papa, I know. You are their father too."

Leonid Ivanovitch chuckled. "That's right. Strange as it may seem, I am their father, not that I have heard either of them address me by that name."

"You won't hear it from me." Madge did not recognize her brother's voice—the tone was so harsh and bitter.

"Because of my work?"

"That's right. You were not born a member of the KGB; you chose to be one."

Leonid Ivanovitch gave a short hard laugh. "A choice? Let me tell you something. It happened during my last year at the university. I was majoring in modern languages, English and French, but I had also picked up enough Greek and Turkish from the merchants and sailors in the port and in the taverns to get along. I was planning to go for a doctorate, and eventually do research in languages. Then one day I was summoned to the KGB headquarters. I confess, I was scared, but when I presented myself I was received as a guest and offered coffee and cognac. I was complimented on my progress at the university and finally offered a good position in their organization."

John started to say something, but Naumov stopped him with a gesture. "I could have refused, of course. Only I was made to understand that if I did not accept the post a good reason would be provided to stop me from graduating. I accepted."

Madge cried, "But aren't you sorry for all those people you send to camps and prisons just because—because"—she frowned, trying to remember her father's exact words—"they protest against something wrong?"

"I am not sorry for them. At the beginning one has qualms, yes, but then one gets used to the game. One has no feelings except sometimes a twinge of envy for those who cannot be bribed or broken into changing their beliefs."

John said stonily, "You had a choice," but his voice was drowned out by Victor's.

"But, Papa, you made me think I could join the KGB when I grew up. And now you said all these things. Why were you giving me all those assignments? I thought you wanted me to practice, to get experience."

"That's a good question." Leonid Ivanovitch sighed. "I suppose I wanted to make it up to you. I neglected you when you were small. After your mother died, I wanted us to become closer. But you were a little old to be taken to the zoo or for an ice cream, and neither of us is keen enough on sports to sit through a soccer match. So I began to give you those assignments, as you call them. I admit that you did a good job. As to following in my footsteps, only time will tell."

"Is that how you found out about us?" Madge asked. "Because Victor followed us to the professor's house?"

"That was the first link. After your visit, I sent my men to search the professor's house. I wondered if they could find any letters from Marina. When they found nothing, I figured Marina must be dead. She is, isn't she?"

Madge nodded. "Yes, giving birth. She was hiding in the hold of a freighter and—and—"

Naumov bit his lip. "Naturally. She was almost eight months pregnant. I thought there might be a possibility that you were Marina's children. Last night I saw you and became sure."

John said defiantly, "But you never acknowledged us. It would have hurt your career to have two children who are American citizens."

For the first time that evening emotion passed over Naumov's face. "No, that was not the reason why I did not say anything to you last night. The reason was I had nothing to offer you in exchange for the life you already have, and I am sure you are old enough to understand that I am not talking about material values."

There was a long silence. Madge broke it by exclaiming, "The manuscript! We have almost forgotten it. Please give it to us."

"Ah, yes, the manuscript. . . ." Stepping back to the table, Naumov took the package and looked at it. His lips became one thin line.

"I can't give it to you," he said. "Giving this manuscript to you would mean it is going to be published abroad. I can't let this happen, even though the contents would be probably nothing new to the West. However, since it did not reach me through official channels, this is what we can do." Removing the brown paper cover, Naumov took the first few pages and tore them in half and then in quarters.

Madge gasped, "No! Please don't!"

Naumov ignored her and Madge did not try to plead with him again.

When the last sheet of paper was destroyed, Leonid Ivanovitch looked up at the twins. "I should also tell you that taking this manuscript with the intent to smuggle it abroad was a foolish thing to do. Had you been caught with this book in your possession, there would have been serious trouble, *very* serious trouble. Even the fact of your being underage would not have helped much. And now"—he glanced at his watch—"I think it is time for you to go."

Victor touched his father's sleeve. "They are not going to stay with us then?" he asked in a whisper.

Naumov shook his head.

Victor's expression was a queer mixture of disappointment and relief.

"May I let you out?" Naumov said to the twins.

There were no good-byes. The door opened and Madge passed through, John after her, and the door closed.

Madge whirled around. "John, we must go back."

"No."

"Yes, we must. You didn't see—he looked so sad. We can't leave him just like that."

"That's exactly what he wanted us to do, *leave.*"

Madge started to knock.

"Are you out of your mind?" John seized her by the shoulders. "Do you want a whole crowd of tenants to gather in here?"

He had barely spoken when the door across the way opened and an elderly woman shuffled out. Coming to Madge, she gently patted her hair. "Were you pleading for someone, girl?" she asked in Russian. "And he refused? Don't try to force your way back. He won't let you in. He's that kind of a man."

"She's right." John took Madge's arm. "Let's go."

"Yes, yes, take her and go in peace," the old woman muttered, going back to her own door.

Madge and John went out onto the landing, then down the stairway. It seemed to Madge that each step was a mile, taking them farther and farther away.

CHAPTER 25

HOMEWARD

"YOU knew all the time," Madge said.

The twins were out of the building and walking toward French Boulevard. "No, not all the time. When I first saw Victor, I thought he reminded me of someone, but it was only a passing impression. Later, when he showed me those snapshots he took with his camera, I saw his father's picture, and something about his face looked familiar to me, but the photograph was blurred and I couldn't be sure. Now, thinking back, I realize that the picture reminded me of you. But it was only after we met Victor in the park that I really knew. Remember how Victor went at Kolia? He threw back his head just like you do when you're mad at someone. Then he took off his glasses, and I couldn't help noticing that he looked like both of us. Those glasses really change his face. I wondered whether you had noticed as well, but you were too busy trying to stop the fight between the two boys."

"You never told me."

"I hoped I was wrong. Still, I almost told you once, on that hot day, when we were sitting in the Douglases' living room. I asked you how you imagined our father. After you described him to me, I did not have the heart to tell you. In fact, I decided right at that moment not to tell you."

"I might have discovered the truth somehow."

"I don't see how you could have, except once—that night when the KGB were in the Bulanovs' apartment and we went

120

down the fire escape. Naumov let us out of the gates. The flashlight shined in his face and I thought you would see the resemblance, but you didn't. If that business with the manuscript had not come up, we would have left for home without your ever suspecting that Naumov was our father." As Madge listened to John, she glanced back at number 3 Uyutnaya for the last time.

"Don't get any ideas about going back," John said, taking her arm.

The twins mingled with the stream of people on the sidewalk. "I hate to think we will probably never see the Bulanovs again," Madge said.

"So do I."

A few minutes later, Madge suddenly said, "John, there's something I want to ask you. You didn't want me to know who our father was, but even when we were still back at home, you were against our looking for him. Why?"

"Why? Didn't you ever wonder why Marina risked her life crossing the ocean in the hold of a freighter when she was eight months pregnant? She had to be escaping from someone. Could it have been her husband? Was she running away from him? This hit me the minute grandfather told us the story, but you just ignored that part. You made a hero of Marina's husband and you clung to that idea."

"I suppose I did."

John was walking faster now, and in spite of herself Madge fell in step with him. "We are going back where we belong, to the States, grandfather, to our friends," he said. "So forget about it."

Madge shook her head. "Home seems so remote to me right now."

"I feel the same way, but it will pass. After we're home for a few days, Odessa will seem remote and our life will go on just as before."

Madge sighed. "No, I think you're wrong. How can things be the same ever again?"